A WARRIOR'S RECKONING

THE AMADÁN
BOOK ONE

BRENNA ASH

A reluctant laird.

Broderick MacLeod never expected to be laird of a clan he hasn't been a part of in years. As a member of the Amadán, a secretive group of mercenaries sworn to exact justice and fight for those who can't, he's accustomed to leading warriors. But being laird is a responsibility he isn't prepared for, and when he finds a brutalized lass on his way back to his childhood home, the need to protect her wars with his duty to his clan, now dependent on him following the untimely deaths of his father and brother. And as they grow closer, the pull of attraction between them is undeniable.

A tormented woman.

Maggie Grant is not some weak maiden that will acquiesce without a fight. After barely surviving being abducted after an attack on her village, she plots her revenge against the vile brute who stole everything from her. Even if it means defying the powerful laird who provided her safety and shelter. The same man who not only earned her hard-won trust, but shows her she is worthy of being loved.

Their quest for vengeance.

Both Maggie and Broderick yearn to deal the death blow to the brigand who has taken everything from them. When their shared enemy threatens not only their happiness, but their lives, can they work together to destroy him? Or will shadows from their past tear apart their future together?

A Warrior's Reckoning
Brenna Ash

Copyright © 2023 by Brenna Ash
Dark Moor Media, LLC

Cover Design: Wicked Smart Designs

ISBN: 978-1-7330367-2-6

To Tom, for not complaining once about all the late nights closed up in my writing cave, and keeping the house up and running when time was too tight. Love you always.

ACKNOWLEDGMENTS

When I first came up with the idea for A Warrior's Reckoning, I didn't think it would be three and a half years before I saw it in print. And there were many times, that I didn't think it would ever make it there.

I have so many people to thank on this one.

Chelle, thanks for talking me down from the ledge when I just wanted to throw in the towel and give up on this book. Your help has been integral in getting this book to the end.

Marie, your words of encouragement and confidence that I can do it have been invaluable and a light in the dark.

SSCG, I'm sorry you had to hear the same chapters over and over again until I got it right. You all have helped and cheered me on from the get go.

Princess Crew, finally, I can move onto the next book!! And you no longer need to listen to me wonder how I'm ever going to get to the end on this one on our writing retreats.

Andrea and Eliza, my Scotland travel buddies. We visited the inspiration for Straik castle on our first Scotland trip and had such a blast exploring all the details!

And of course, my family. Without your support, I wouldn't be able to do this job that I love so much.

CHAPTER 1

Sandaig, Highlands, Scotland
1482

 aggie Grant awoke with a start, causing an intense pain to lance through her head at the sudden movement. Her hands were bound at the wrist, and she was laying upon something hard.

Where was she? Was she moving? She must be. That was definitely the muffled sound of hooves pounding the ground. What had happened? Because it felt like someone had taken a broadsword to her head.

Her mind was muddled, as if she'd partaken of too much ale. She opened her eyes but saw nothing. Complete darkness. Stiff, rough material scratched at her face, irritating her tender skin. Was there a woolen hood upon her head? Is that what blocked her view.

What the bloody hell was happening?

She stretched her neck to see if she could hear anything

that would give her any indication as to where she was. It was eerily silent except for the horses' hooves slapping the ground and a slight rustling as wind filtered through the surrounding trees and caused the branches to rub against each other.

She'd recognize the sound anywhere. It reminded her of the walks she used to take with her father through the woods in the late days of fall, before the attack on their village. But *where* was she? Mayhap in those same woods, and if she was lucky, close to her home. Had they returned her to where they'd taken her from?

Diel would never be so kind.

Slowly, the puzzle pieces began to click together. She and her captor, Diel, had been in her room—no, her dungeon— when one of his men came in and told him he'd received a missive. To her relief, he'd left the room, but a few minutes later a group of his men entered. Grabbing her arms roughly, they'd yanked her from her prison. She didn't bother to scream—there was no one that would come to her aid. She struggled to keep up as they dragged her through the dark halls of the castle and out the massive door.

It had been the first glimpse she'd had outside of the sorrowful place she'd been kept in since they'd taken her from her home. That massive structure had loomed above her, its exterior darkened by the green moss that grew in large patches up the sides of the stone walls. Its outward appearance was equal to the man who owned it. Cold, dark, and foreboding. How far away was it from the village she'd spent her whole life in?

Outside the castle, one of the men had grasped her by the chin and forced her to look at him. His leering grin sent shivers down her spine. He was almost as frightening as Diel. Just as tall, with evil eyes, though his were a chilling blue compared to Diel's swamp-colored eyes.

"Smile, sunshine," he had sneered. "Yer wish has been granted. We've orders to release ye."

She couldn't remember anything after that. They must have hit her, knocking her out.

Now, the smell of pine infiltrated through the musty-smelling hood. The soft rustle of leaves carried on the cool night breeze. They were definitely in the forest. She prayed it was the forest near her home, that these were the same pine trees she'd tried running towards to evade capture.

They were riding, she knew that much, for her body bounced in time to the pounding of a horse's cantering hooves. A man held her in a death grip, his fingers painfully digging into her skin.

She shivered. Cold seeped into her sore bones.

Maggie stiffened at the close proximity of the man behind her. As uncomfortable as the position was, at least her hands acted as a small barrier between them so he couldn't push himself fully against her back. Though she dared not move them for fear of coming in contact with a part of him she wanted naught to do with.

The rider made no move to touch her other than to hold her in place. He wouldn't dare—Diel was a selfish beast. He'd marked her as his and only his. For a time, she had fought hard with everything in her, but in the end, his strength was too much for her to overcome.

He'd ravaged her body one time. One time.

It wouldn't happen again. She'd die first.

Though she called her captor Diel she didn't truly know his name. Diel, *the devil*. A description never more befitting someone so vile. He was not a man. He was a monster.

He and his men had raided her village nights ago. She couldn't remember how many days exactly, though it seemed like a lifetime. How far had they taken her from the village she'd spent her whole life in?

"Look who's finally awake," the man said, his mouth close to her ear.

Maggie jerked her head to the right to get away from him, but his grip held, and he laughed.

A whistle sounded from one of the other men and the horses came to a stop. Yanked roughly from her mount, Maggie tumbled down, landing hard on the ground. Her bare feet sank into the damp earth, the sharp caps of acorns pricking at the soles of her feet.

Why had they brought her here? In the days since Diel had taken her captive, she'd never been allowed outside. Maybe now that he'd gotten what he wanted, her captor had decided he'd had enough. Was this how her life ended?

Her shoulders sagged in defeat. They'd been lying to her when they'd said they were letting her go. She'd been through so much, bore the scars of Diel's torture upon her body and her soul.

Now they'd kill her. At least she would be reunited with her family and friends. Those that lost their lives at Diel's hand. She could find solace in that. Couldn't she?

No.

I must survive. I must avenge them. I will not allow their deaths to be forgotten.

Her emotions roiled to the surface. A niggling voice repeated those words of defiance in her head. She would not lay down and die. Would not allow her loved ones to die in vain. There had to be a way out of this. She would damn Diel and his men to Hell first, but she would not give them the satisfaction of giving up. Her da had taught her better than that. Hell, she was stronger than that. If there was a chance for escape, she had to take it. *She would take it.* But it was impossible for her to form a plan without being able to see her surroundings.

The darkness was her newest enemy.

Since no one was holding her at the moment, she rose to her full height and tentatively took a step forward.

Oof. A hard, unmoving body stopped her advance. Beefy, calloused hands grasped her bare shoulders and steadied her.

"Just where do ye think ye're going?" The sneering voice belonged to the same man she'd shared a horse with.

Maggie had to do something. She hadn't fought Diel so strongly and survived his torture for her life to end like this.

She did the only thing she could think of in the moment. Heaving in a chest full of air, she opened her mouth and set forth the loudest war cry she could muster. One even she didn't know she was capable of. The thin wool of the hood was no match for the anger and desperation in her powerful voice, its purpose relegated to the sole task of barring her sight. She was roughly shoved away as her high-pitched scream echoed through the trees. Her bum hit the ground with a thud, putting an abrupt end to her cry.

"Damn it, wench," he bent and hissed near her ear. "I said 'twas yer lucky day. Dinna make me change my mind."

Hooves sounded in the distance and she

Someone grabbed the bindings around her wrists and hauled her roughly against them. She tried not to flinch, and instead focused on the men moving around her. She listened intently but still didn't know what was happening. Twigs cracked under the men's boots and the horses huffed and whinnied, impatient to run off.

Her breath quickened, but she dared not move. Not yet.

Maggie would have to do something soon if she were to have any hope of escape. She could tell by their differing voices there were at least three of them. How in the world was she supposed to get away from three grown men on horses? A hard knee to the groin of one, and a left hook to the jaw of another. It was worth a try. Truly she had no other choice.

It seemed impossible.

No, she silently scolded herself.

She simply had to find the right time. The perfect moment to strike, because she wouldn't get a second chance. Regardless of whether she succeeded or not, she wouldn't go down without a fight.

All she needed was a fighting chance. Her very life depended on it.

Maggie concentrated on their voices and the heat emanating from their bodies. She said a silent prayer. Just as she got the courage to make her move the sounds of hooves pounded in her ears.

A wet, mossy scent filtered through the hood and into her nose and she felt clumps of damp earth slap against her bare legs.

Were they leaving? There was no way she could be so lucky. But it sure sounded like it. She could no longer hear the snorting of the horses or the men talking to one another. The noises ebbed until the only sounds other than Maggie's breathing were the creatures sharing the night with her.

Disbelief at whether they'd left her made her remain still. Freedom felt false.

Instinct kicked in. She should run. Had to run. But how far would she get with her hands bound and this damned hood on her head? She couldn't see anything. With her luck, she'd likely run full force into a tree and knock herself out.

Maggie needed to think, but most of all she needed to move. Twisting her wrists back and forth she tried to undo her binds and was surprised to find that they had been loosened. The man who had grabbed her must have done it. Thank God for small blessings. She slipped one hand free then the other and the binds fell to the ground. She rubbed her wrists and winced at the fiery pain where the skin had been chafed and rubbed raw.

Maggie tore the hood off her head and sucked in a lungful of fresh air. She turned toward the direction she believed the horses had gone, narrowed her eyes, and surveyed the darkness.

Nothing. Had her prayers been answered, and they'd truly left her alone? Or were they toying with her?

She had to find a place to hide as far away from this spot as she could. Because she'd be damned if she waited for them to come back for her.

Just as she was about to dash into the dense brush, she noticed a folded square of wool laying on the ground at her feet. It wasn't from her shift, though it had been ripped in several places.

What was it?

It must have fallen out of one of the men's bags. Would she be granted one more miracle today? Could this be something of worth that she could barter with? Maybe to pay for protection. She wouldn't survive very long out here alone since she had minimal means to protect herself.

She unfolded the piece of wool and held it up toward the scant light glinting through the trees. A startled breath escaped when the moonlight glittered off a beautiful, expensive-looking brooch.

Maggie couldn't make out the actual design in the limited light, but it would surely come in handy, as someone would undoubtedly pay a hefty amount for it. If she were lucky, it might even help her learn Diel's true identity and lead her to him. It was hard to destroy a man if she didn't know who he was.

Hopefully this brooch would lead her to him. She picked up the small piece of brown wool, rough in texture. Its length was barely wide enough to cover her shoulders, so she wrapped it around her neck. Other than her shift, it was the only protection she had against the dank chill of the night.

Maggie tapped into her anger, drew a deep breath to fill her lungs and stopped when pain lanced her breast. Diel's last beating had been especially brutal. No matter. She would take a thousand beatings over the violation of her innocence.

Nightmarish thoughts froze her in place, unable to take even a small step. She squeezed her eyes tight, shook her head, and shoved the memories into that place in her mind where they would be locked away with all the others.

Diel thought he could beat her into submission. Make her bow down to him.

He was dead wrong. Everything he did to her solidified her determination to seek revenge.

Fear now mixed with vengeance and spurred her forward. Maggie focused on her surroundings. Turning in what she hoped was the opposite direction the men had rode off to, she sprinted as fast as her legs would allow. Terror that they could come back at any moment urged her to push forward past the pain and continue on.

Surrounded by darkness, with no knowledge of where she was, she ran through the trees, ignoring the sticks and sharp stones as they cut into the bottoms of her feet, looking for any signs of life. Though, she'd probably exceeded her fair share of miracles, she hoped to stumble on a village or a hut.

An owl hooted nearby, startling her, causing her heart to skip a beat. Its eerie cry sent cold tingles down her spine. Cold seeped into her bones. Her thin shift offered little to no protection from the elements, and the small length of wool provided small comfort as she trekked forward. Still, she put one foot in front of the other, knowing that if she didn't keep moving, she would freeze to death.

She shivered not only from the cold, but with the knowledge that the woods were not a safe place for a lass.

Especially at night.

She had no idea who or what might be lurking in these woods. Stalking her. Watching her every move. Or which creature was more dangerous—the two-legged or four-legged kind?

Her desperation to find a village drove her forward and still there was nothing. No place to offer her solace or protect from monsters like Diel.

Maggie didn't even know whose lands she was on. She had no concept of how far they had ridden or for how long. She knew nothing of her former captor, other than his brutish demeanor.

He and his men had attacked her village under the cover of night. Her heart ached at the memory. The shrieks of her people. The smell of smoke stinging her nostrils as their quaint thatch homes burned to the ground. Bairns calling for their mamas. Wives yelling for their husbands, who were trying to fight off the invaders to no avail. The attackers were too strong and too great in number. They were fighters. Warriors. Her village of farmers and merchants were no match against such a force.

Maggie could still hear their screams. Her mama's yell for her to 'run!'. Being no match for the attackers, she'd sprinted toward the trees.

As she tried to escape the invaders, she'd stumbled over corpses, falling upon them to meet their open, unseeing eyes. Their lifeblood stone from them by raiding pillagers. The bodies of the slain—her friends and neighbors-- scattered over the grounds of the village were forever emblazoned in her memory.

Maggie was sure there were no survivors, that her parents had been murdered. She was the only one left.

Diel had captured her as she ran toward the woods, hooking his arm around her neck and dragging her onto his war horse. The black-haired heathen had tossed her roughly on the huge beast before mounting behind her. It was still a mystery why he hadn't dispensed with her like all the others.

Why had he let her live?

Lost in thought, she didn't notice a low hanging branch, and hissed as the sharp wood gouged the skin of her cheek. It was the same place she'd cut Diel when trying to escape his arms. She'd been holding a small dagger when he'd wrestled her onto his horse. Instinctively, she'd slashed out at him with a vicious slice that ran from his temple to his jawline.

He'd cursed loudly, his dark eyes became almost black in color, and he tore the knife from her grasp. He'd drawn back his hand and slapped her hard enough her teeth rattled.

Maggie took pride in that cut and took solace in knowing he would carry that scar until the end of his days. Someday, she would identify him by that scar, and then, she would kill him.

Since that time, her days had been filled with naught but misery.

But tonight—tonight was the first time in as many nights she felt a wee smidge of hope. Maybe God had shined his light down on her and taken pity on her dire situation.

Whatever the reason, Maggie needed to make haste.

Her toes were cold, pain causing them to cramp and making it hard to keep moving. Blood seeped from previous wounds exacerbated by stepping over sharp rocks. The cuts would become festered if she didn't come upon water soon to tend to them.

No, she couldn't stop.

What if Diel changed his mind and sent his men back out to capture her again. What if all this was a ruse and they only gave her a head start and would soon hunt her down like a dog?

She needed to get as far away as possible, to find a place to hide, but it was harder than she thought to get her bearings. The pine trees all looked the same and it was so dark she couldn't tell if she was running in circles. She took in a settling breath, looking to the moon to calm her, and focused on the sounds of the night. All she heard was her breathing and some forest animals shuffling through the brush. No men stalking her. No horses' hooves pounding toward her. Just the occasional owl, and perhaps the mournful call of a wolf in the distance. That was a beastie she did *not* want to cross paths with.

Her lungs burned from the cold and feet protested with each rock, thorn, or pinecone she stepped upon. It felt like she had been running for hours, but the sky was still dark. The only glimmer of light was the silvery streams sneaking down through the tree branches high overhead.

Maggie decided to let the moon's glow be her guide.

No matter how tired she was or how much her bones ached, and her thighs burned, she pushed forward. Refused to stop. Unsure whether she was moving closer to Diel's land, if it even was his, or if she was moving in the opposite direction. Hopefully, the latter, but who knew?

She had always regretted not venturing far from her home, never more than this moment. Her parents had been simple merchants who didn't travel, except for her father. He had on a few occasions traveled to visit with the laird. Even so, for the most part, none of them were familiar with lands outside of their village.

Until the day Diel and his band of heathens attacked, they had led a quiet, happy life. Maggie had helped with the upkeep of their small, thatch-roofed hut, and assisted her parents when they would sell their wares around the village.

The village was all she'd ever known.

Now it was gone.

Her parents and every other person she'd ever loved, were gone.

The realization hit her anew. She was alone.

Diel had ripped away everything that mattered to her. He'd taken the one thing that should have been hers to give. Not something that was stolen from her with such violence.

She still had her life, and she was grateful to the fates for intervening. Now, she could avenge those she'd lost, and punish Diel for the torment he'd inflicted upon her.

Overcome with emotion, Maggie sank to her knees. A mixture of fear, disgust…and, finally, relief washed over her. Whatever it took, she would find that carefree girl she once was.

Even free of Diel, the scars would always be there, written upon her body and her heart. Also newly carved into her mind, body, and soul was that she was a survivor. That she had been blessed with a life, with a future. She would use every last breath she had to find Diel and make him suffer.

Dampness began to seep through the thin cloth of her shift, and the cold crept through her body. She hadn't slept well since her capture and was so very tired. Terror that Diel would come into her room at night to do the unthinkable had denied her the escape of sleep. Instead, she lay on the floor in the corner furthest from the door, always watching, listening, waiting for footsteps to approach. Every time she heard boots on the stone, her body stiffened, and she struggled to breathe. Once they passed her door, the relief she'd felt had been immense, and it would take some time for her heart to slow its pounding. It was impossible to sleep with that fear every night.

Tears fell from her eyes, the liquid warm as it rolled along her cheeks before landing in the soil and leaves.

Enough Maggie.

She was done wallowing in her own misery. She would not give Diel the satisfaction. Drawing her shoulders back and, needing to carry on, she pressed her hands into the mud and tried to stand. Her knees buckled and she hit the ground hard.

Frustrated and angry at herself for her weakness, she pounded her fists into the earth and wept. Sobs loud enough to wake the dead were wrenched from her gut. She drew her knees up, wrapped her arms around them, and rolled to her side on the ground.

"This will not be my end," Maggie uttered the oath into the night air. "I did not survive Diel's cruelty to die alone in these woods."

She would take a wee respite—only long enough to gather her strength. Then she would awake refreshed and carry on.

Diel and his men abandoned her thinking she would die out here alone in the forest.

The fools.

She would live to spite them and their laird.

This is their fault.

Diel had taken everything from her, but she was not to blame. Not only would she survive, but she would also make the bastard pay for all he'd done. To her parents. To her friends. To her village.

To her.

He would pay for the total destruction he'd exacted on the innocent and happy life she'd known.

But she couldn't do that while she was so, so tired.

Her eyes grew heavy, and she cursed aloud the man who created this situation, wishing upon him the most heinous death when his time came. As sleep pulled her into its embrace, she smiled knowing she would be the one to land the death blow.

CHAPTER 2

*B*roderick MacLeod glanced up at the darkening sky and muttered a curse.

Luck had not been on his side these past few weeks. He'd been traveling to Inverness to undertake his latest Amadán mission when the missive from Alastair Lewis had arrived, calling him back to his childhood home. In the letter, the Amadán leader and the man who had been more of a father to him than his own flesh and blood, had ended with the words: "Ye're laird now. Come home."

"Home," he spat.

Straik hadn't been his home for years. Not since he was a young lad. It had stopped being so the day his dear mother passed.

His heart skipped a beat at the thought of his mum. A beautiful and kind woman who had deserved so much more than the overbearing brute she'd spent the best years of her life with.

As if reflecting his mood, the gray clouds hung low, moving swiftly to bring in the rain that threatened to fall before night came. He could smell the change in the heavy autumn air. He was still at least a day's ride from his father's castle.

No. Straik Castle was *his* now.

A change in circumstances he'd not foreseen. His older brother, Ewan, was supposed to be the next laird of Straik. From the moment he was born, Ewan had been trained for the position as head of the MacLeod. Callum, their father, had taught Ewan how to lead. How to handle the clan.

Broderick, as the second son, was just an afterthought. A disappointment to his now dead father. A laughingstock to his brother, also dead.

Both men had been killed a fortnight ago. Ambushed on a wild boar hunt by an unknown attacker. Each taking an arrow to the chest. Now, as his first act as laird, Broderick would need to find out who had killed them. And once he did, he'd make damn sure the attackers paid with their lives. His clansmen would expect nothing less.

A gust of wind lifted his hair off his shoulders and blew the blond strands into his face. Leaning forward, he gave his horse Goliath's neck a pat and swung his leg over the side and dropped to the ground.

Reins in hand, he led his horse over to a tree and secured the massive beast so he could have a look around and decide where would be the best spot to set up camp for the night. A copse of trees several lengths from the road would provide the needed shelter from the rain that was just now starting to fall in big drops, plopping to the ground with a splatter. Damn rain. The road would be a muddy mess to travel on the morrow. Fitting.

He moved Goliath under the trees to keep him out of the rain and then laid his plaid out on the ground. Untying the satchel from his belt, he grabbed a crust of bread and a hunk of cheese. Breaking the bread in half, he held his hand out to Goliath and waited for the horse as he took a loud sniff and then gently ate out of his palm. Broderick had run out of the horse bread; the oat, wheat, and rye concoction Goliath enjoyed overly much. His bread would have to suffice until they made it to Straik and he could get a proper feeding in.

"Ye're a fine beast, Goliath." As if understanding him, the horse nuzzled his hand before letting out a huff of air. "Aye, 'tis going to be a long night."

Broderick gave him a final pat and sat on his plaid, ignoring the rough and bumpy ground with its twigs jabbing the underside of his thighs through his trews, and finished his meal.

The area was fairly dry. The trees did a good job of stopping the rain from coming through, but he'd still need a fire to combat the chill of the night. He gathered small branches and brush and piled them together in a small circle of stones he'd arranged. It didn't take long before the fire roared to life. Using the satchel to rest his head upon, Broderick wrapped the plaid around his shoulders and closed his eyes.

He and his mentor Alastair had much to discuss—the attack on his father and brother, first and foremost. They would also need to assign someone else to the Inverness mission. That was to be Broderick's latest mission for the Amadán—the band of warrior brothers created and led by Alastair. The group townsfolk whispered about across Scotland, almost as if they were a myth. Anonymity was their goal, and they'd achieved that, since their existence was always questioned.

Rest assured, they *were* real.

Each member performed their duties in secret. Infiltrating clans. Waiting for the right time to strike, and then meting out deserved justice that those of the underprivileged couldn't do. They fought for what was right and just. Morals and ethics were important within the Amadán.

Broderick was one of the senior warriors and he hadn't

lost a mission yet. This last one not included. It wasn't his decision to be taken off and summoned to his childhood home. Being called back irritated him. He would much rather be in Inverness, making inroads with the clan and studying the laird to see if he truly was planning an uprising. Now that job would fall to someone else since he had a duty to his own clan. One he would fulfill, but he wouldn't be happy about it.

In the morning, he'd push Goliath to get them to Straik Castle as soon as possible. He wanted to get off the roads and deal with his father and brother's affairs as soon as possible.

The long ride had made him weary, and his eyes grew heavy, his heart calmed by the slight rustle of the leaves clinging to the branches. He'd just begun to drift off to sleep when he heard it.

The faintest whisper of a curse spoken in the wind and carried through the trees. Sitting up, he listened, but didn't hear it again.

Still, he'd swear an oath he'd heard something. A woman.

Was it his head playing games on him? He needed to know. Sleep all but forgotten, he stood and stroked Goliath's mane. "Did ye hear that?"

The horse huffed, but otherwise ignored Broderick.

"I'm going to take a walk. Ye dinna go anywhere whilst I'm gone." He gave the horse a final pat and headed in the direction where he'd thought the voice had come from.

What would possess a woman to be in these woods after nightfall? Was she alone? Lost? The fallen pine needles covering the forest floor muffled his steps as he made his way through the birch and spruce trees, listening for anything that would give a hint to where she may be.

He was just about to turn and make his way back to Goliath when he heard a sniffle, as though she were crying?

He moved forward, around a huge pine tree, and saw her. Curled into a ball on the cold ground lay a lass.

"Lass?" Broderick rushed to the woman and dropped to his knees beside her. "Are ye ill?"

In the filtered light of the moon he could see her back was to him, and she was only wearing a shift.

Gently, he placed a hand on her shoulder, he didn't want to startle her.

She didn't move.

"Lass?"

She remained silent. Was she alive? He held his breath at the same time he listened to hear hers. Eyes closed, he concentrated, waited, and after a few moments, there it was.

A shallow breath. Rickety. But it was there.

She wasn't dead yet, and he'd be damned if she'd die on his watch.

He moved around so he could face the lass and his blood boiled at the sight. Her exact age was impossible to ascertain as her face was a mass of marks and cuts. Her eyes were swollen, black and blue. She'd been beaten badly, perhaps more than once. Bruises, purple and angry covered her cheeks. Blood mixed with mud, matted her hair to her skin and the earth beneath her.

"Jesus," he cursed. Who the hell could do such a thing? And how, pray tell, did she get in the woods?

The thin shift she wore did nothing to protect her from the elements of the harsh early autumn weather. The damp material clung to her thin body and Broderick seethed even more when he saw the dark-colored bruises that covered her legs, where the fabric didn't cover her skin.

He gently lifted her into his arms—the poor thing was just skin and bones. He had to get her in front of the fire to warm her up.

She let out a small cry as Broderick cradled her closer.

"Shh, lass. Ye're safe now." He quickly made his way through the trees and back to where he'd set up camp. Carrying her was an easy task. Her weight so slight that she must have been wandering around in the woods for days.

Goliath neighed and stomped a hoof when Broderick returned, seeming to acknowledge the lass now with him.

Settling by the fire, Broderick was careful not to crush her with his weight as he sat. A wee moan escaped from her swollen, cracked lips as he carefully wrapped his plaid around her for warmth. She was so frail. Her bones pushed against her skin, threatening to break through the thin barrier with no meat to pad them. She continued to shiver, even in front of the fire swaddled in his plaid. Not only cold, but she must also be starving. But she seemed to have fainted before he'd found her and hadn't woken up yet.

He needed to get her to Straik as soon as possible so she could see the healer. Traveling before first light was out of the question. He just had to try to keep her warm for the night.

Tomorrow, they'd make haste for Straik. He couldn't give her the care she needed out here. He didn't have the supplies required to tend to her wounds nor the knowledge. She was no warrior sliced in a fight where he could administer a crude line of stitches. Nay, she required more help than that. He looked down at the lass.

With his ability to help her hampered, he prayed for first light to arrive quickly.

THE RAIN LASTED through the night and still fell in a soft mist the next morning when Broderick packed up his few items to leave. It was just after dawn and he was itching to get moving.

He'd spent the night with his arms wrapped around the lass, trying to shield her from the cold rain with his body heat. It wasn't much, but she'd made it through the night.

She hadn't awakened and was lying where he'd left her by the fire allowing him a moment so he could hurriedly clean up camp.

The fire had gone out just before daybreak, but he still ran his boot through the soot, crushing any embers that may have lingered. The woods were alive with the sing-song tweets of the chaffinches as they flitted about the trees, hopping from one branch to another, chasing each other as if they had no other care in the world. Their carefreeness the opposite of the fearfulness the lass must have felt—right until the moment she'd collapsed.

Though she was still asleep, he hoped that her dream-world was safe. He prayed that she could somehow sense that she was safe now. That he was here and wouldn't let any further harm come to her.

He bent and cradled the woman in his left arm as he carefully mounted Goliath. She stirred at the jostling and moaned softly. Even her moan sounded pained.

"Shh, 'tis okay, lass. I've got ye." He settled her on his lap, and she didn't make another sound. His gut twisted with worry. He'd done what he could for her through the night, but it didn't help in the way of treating her wounds. She was in dire need of a healer. Straik would have one. At least it had when he was younger and lived there.

He squeezed his calves into Goliath's sides and the horse, as if knowing he was carrying precious cargo, tentatively broke into a slow trot.

The lass was quiet as the dead. Broderick retracted that thought as soon as it entered in his mind. She would not die. He would get her to Straik and nurse her back to health.

And then when she was healthy enough, he'd find out

who the bastard was that had brutalized her so. Broderick would track him down and skin him alive after giving him the same treatment he'd inflicted upon the lass.

His whole life he'd meted out justice to those that deserved it. As a member of the Amadán, he usually was paid a hefty fee for his efforts. This one he'd do at no cost.

Pulling his plaid tighter around her, he rested his free arm around her shoulders, and his fingers brushed against her chestnut brown hair. At least he believed that was the color. It was hard to tell with so much dirt and blood stuck to it.

They were both in dire need of baths once they finally made their arrival.

The lass seemed to be taking the journey well, so he kicked Goliath into a faster trot. He had her braced safely against him, to ensure he took the brunt of the bumps of the journey for her.

The caws and calls of the birds were the only sounds other than the pounding of Goliath's hooves on the muddied dirt of the road.

His thoughts wandered, mainly to stop him from worrying about the lass overmuch. He already knew how he would be received by his clan.

Unkindly. Or at least with indifference.

Why would they treat him any other way? His clansmen hadn't seen him for years. And up until the last year or so he'd been at Straik, he'd been a weak boy. Nothing more than an outlet for his father to take out his frustrations on. The beatings he'd endured when he was a lad. He'd never forgotten them. Vowed never to find himself in that position again. He looked down at the lass and was assaulted with memories he'd buried long ago. No one deserved to be mistreated so.

His life changed when Alastair came to live with them after his family had been killed. His father's cousin, the man treated Broderick like the son he'd lost. With a love he'd never received from his own father.

Broderick had left Straik as soon as he was able. Under Alastair's mentorship, he was introduced to the Amadán, and he spent hours a day training. He was soon one of the physically strongest members of the group. Each mission he was assigned, he threw himself into the task full force. His skill with a bow was nothing to look down upon, but his skill with a sword? Now that was something to talk about.

And people had. He'd made a fair amount of coin fighting his way through the countryside. Since the members of the Amadán were secret, Callum and Ewan only ever heard of Broderick's prowess and strength in known paid missions. But he was satisfied, knowing his father was hearing of his escapades and cringing. It had given Broderick a deep sense of pride that he'd made a name for himself. Something his father had said he'd never do.

He hadn't become the disappointment his father had always claimed he would be. Though now he'd lost the chance to tell his father as much. He didn't dwell on that fact. If he'd really wanted to tell him, Broderick could have come home any time and done so.

The lass shifted on his lap and cried out, trying to sit up.

"Shh, lass."

Instinctively, Goliath slowed.

The lass looked up at him and her skin seemed to pale even more. Something he didn't think was possible.

There was such fear in her eyes. All he wanted to do was help her understand that he would never do anything to hurt her. But he didn't think now was the time for long explanations.

"I'm no' going to hurt ye, lass. I'm taking ye to a healer."

He wasn't sure if she'd heard or understood him. Or if she'd just fainted once more, but she went limp in his arms once again. His brows furrowed in concern. They need to get to Straik quickly. He squeezed Goliath's sides and the horse moved to a gallop. Broderick prayed the lass could hold on until they arrived.

Broderick's mind wandered back to the past as they moved forward to Straik.

The rain had finally stopped misting and the gray clouds were starting to break apart, allowing the sun to peek through. A glimpse of brighter things to come.

He looked down at the lass, his heart breaking for what she'd gone through, and wished only brighter days for her future. He'd work to make that happen for her. Especially during her stay at Straik. Just because the place was a dark memory for him, didn't mean that it needed to be for her.

People could change. Places could too.

He'd never thought about coming back home and making amends. Had he cursed his father and brother? Oh, aye. He'd never forget the hurt he felt seeing the difference in the way Callum treated Broderick compared to the way he treated Ewan.

But they hadn't deserved to die. He would never have wished that fate upon them.

They were gone now, and no memories could be changed. Yet, he vowed to the Heavens that he would avenge their deaths. It was his duty to the clan that he now found himself the leader of. Unexpected as these turns of events were, he would do what was now expected of him. He would find out who had ambushed them, and the murderer would pay.

With their holdings, their coffers, and their lives.

CHAPTER 3

$\mathcal{M}$aggie woke to being jostled about.

She was no longer cold like she was when she'd collapsed. Warmth soaked into her bones. She tried to sit up, however a soothing, but familiar, voice told her not to move. Something about the rider—for she was surely moving on a horse—made her feel safe. But who was it? Unlike the ride she'd suffered before being left in the woods, this ride was cushioned, and the man who held her gentle.

Desperate to see who had found her, Maggie willed her eyes to open, but they wouldn't cooperate. She let out a small cry of frustration.

"Shh, lass. All is well," a kind voice reassured her and the warm blanket she was nestled in tightened around her.

She burrowed into its warmth, finding safety in the way it enveloped her. A wall between her and the outside world. Even as her body tried to sink into that cocoon, her head warned her against a false sense of security. Without seeing her surroundings how could she be certain she was truly safe? She tried desperately to open her eyes again, but to no avail and soon, she felt that shroud of heaviness taking over and her awareness starting to slip away.

The noises around her faded. The thump of the horse's hooves as it stomped into the earth with each step. The songs of the chaffinches as they chittered amongst the trees. The rustle of the leaves. It all grew quieter and quieter, until there was nothing but silence.

Darkness took hold and, for the first time in a long time, she wasn't afraid.

BRODERICK'S MEMORIES kept his mind occupied the rest of his journey as he pushed Goliath to his limits. His horse badly needed rest, but Broderick was determined to get to Straik today and by the time he entered MacLeod lands, he was in a bitter mood.

Not only was he theoretically entering enemy territory—for they didn't know who he was—he now had an unknown lass in tow. He didn't think she would be any more of a welcome sight than he was.

A telltale whistle sounded in the air as he ventured farther into his clan's lands. Similar to the chirp of a bird. If one weren't a MacLeod, they would think nothing of it. But Broderick recognized the alert whistle. Though after so many years, he would have thought they would have changed the signal. At least the clan still had their guards posted.

He slowed, well aware that at any moment at least two men would show themselves, questioning why they were here.

As if on cue, two armed guards stepped out of the woods and stood in front of him while two more dropped from the trees onto the ground at Goliath's rear. One of the guards in front of him put his arm up, stopping his progression.

Pulling on Goliath's reins, Broderick halted his horse. Hand on the hilt of his sword, he shifted so he could protect the lass.

These were his men, but if they attacked, he wouldn't hesitate to take them down.

With time of the essence, he couldn't tarry and play a game of cat and mouse. He must get past them and to the castle. But he didn't want the guards to get antsy with their arrows and let them fly, so for the moment he stayed still.

"For what reason have ye entered MacLeod lands?" asked the same guard.

Broderick studied the two men. He didn't recognize either of them, though that wasn't surprising. He looked over his shoulder at the two guards behind him. Neither of them was familiar either.

Just as they did not know him. He'd changed drastically from the boy he'd been when he'd left all those years ago.

"I'm Broderick MacLeod. I've been summoned home by Alastair Lewis. *Ion-dubh,*" he called out, stating the code word Alastair had included in his letter 'to let them know ye are ye' he'd written. It meant blackbird, but Broderick didn't have time to decipher its meaning.

The guard's eyes widened in disbelief.

"Ye came. We werena sure ye would." The guard who seemed to be their spokesman, dipped his head in a slight bow and the others followed suit. "Ye favor yer mother," he said as he studied Broderick's face.

"Aye. We can discuss the reason later. I've naught time for this. The lass needs a healer. She's badly wounded."

"We were always told Duff would take over the position of laird if anything were to ever happen to Callum and Ewan." The man's eyes lingered on the lass a moment before returning to him.

Broderick's jaw tightened at the name of his childhood

nemesis. Duff MacDonald was the second son his father had really wanted. Even as a lad, being fostered at Straik, Duff had shown a cruel streak that fell in line with Callum's way of ruling with fear and manipulation amongst his warriors.

He was not surprised they expected Duff to step up to lead the clan. An issue he would rectify later.

"We always thought that odd." The guard looked to the man next to him who nodded in agreement. "That wasna proper protocol."

Mayhap the clan wasn't looking towards Duff's impending leadership. "'Tis something for a later time—after I get the lass to the healer."

The guard's eyes slid back to the lass.

"What happened?" He approached and reached out a hand to touch the woman.

"Dinna touch the lass." Broderick warned, his voice low.

The guard snapped his hand back, as if afraid to be bitten.

The lass let out a small moan and stirred on his lap.

Broderick glanced down at her, but her eyes were still closed, and she made no further movement.

"I dinna have time to explain. I must make haste. The lass could die." Goliath huffed and threw his head back, stomping his hooves into the ground, as if the beast understood the conversation exchanged between them. "Ye dinna want that on yer conscience." He reached out to stroke the horse's neck in reassurance.

The lass shifted at the horse's sudden movement and a pained cry escaped her lips.

Broderick tightened his hold on her in what he hoped was a reassurance to her and pierced the guard with a look that let the man know he was not being foolhardy.

The guard seemed to understand Broderick's meaning.

"Stand down!" he barked. "Welcome home, my laird. Best

wishes for the lass. The healer will see that she is well cared for."

Broderick didn't wait to hear if he had anything else to say. He'd deal with the guard situation and the matter of updated security later, once the lass was being tended to. He needed to get her to the healer without further delay.

Saying no more, he kicked Goliath into a fast trot past the men and made his way to the bailey of the castle he hadn't seen in years. One he'd thought he'd never see again.

The acceptance of the guards gave him a small glimmer of hope. He really hadn't known what to expect once he'd crossed back onto MacLeod lands. The code word surely helped, but maybe he would have an easier time than he had originally expected with his clansmen.

His clansmen.

It didn't sound right to his own ears.

He'd still have to fight hard to gain the trust of a clan he'd never had any intention or desire to lead. Actions of the past, by both he and his father would not make it easy. Especially if they expected Duff to be their new laird.

He cringed at the thought.

If Duff was anything like he'd been when they were younger, the clan would have a rude awakening when he showed his true, cruel colors.

Broderick didn't think Duff had shown his father his true self. Callum may have been a tough leader, mayhap manipulative at times, but he wasn't outright cruel. Nay, he left that for his family. But he was well liked by the clan, and they respected him. Broderick found it highly doubtful the clan would feel the same way about Duff.

The guards' reaction to his arrival could mean that mayhap the clan knew Duff better than he thought and were not interested in his type of leadership. Which surely would have led to much more war and uncertainty.

At this point, the only way Duff could claim leadership to Clan MacLeod was if Broderick was dead as well. Surely, much to the disappointment of Duff, Broderick was alive and well. The clan didn't belong to Duff, and Broderick would make sure to remind him of that.

He had no intention of leading with brutality. If he was going to be forced into the position, he would make sure that his clansmen were well-cared for and didn't fear their laird.

As he neared the keep, showing its age by the weathered stone, but otherwise looking much the same as when Broderick had last seen it, he ignored the stables that were off to the left and pushed Goliath forward to the inner bailey. An eager young lad with a mass of unruly red curls atop his head met Broderick as he carefully dismounted his horse while still cradling the lass.

"Would ye like me to take care of him fer ye, sir?"

"Leave him for now. Go fetch the healer, quickly!"

The boy's chin lifted way up to take in Broderick and his green eyes widened.

"Go now!" Broderick's voice stirred him into action.

The boy turned and ran toward the castle.

Broderick followed, looking at the lass and noting she looked even paler than she had earlier. He could only pray he wasn't too late.

His long strides carried him to the Great Hall where an elderly woman rushed forth. He was glad to see Orna's familiar face. Her forehead was creased even more and deeper than the last time he'd seen the healer. He'd believed the woman to be old when he was a boy. Now, she was positively ancient.

"What has happened?" Worry accompanied her words.

"The lady has been brutalized. I found her in the woods last night and she has barely said a word. A few moans and groans. Her breath was verra shallow then, but it seems better now. Though I fear her fright is keeping her mind shut down."

Orna nodded. "Come, come." She hurried ahead of him, surprisingly amble for her age. "We're preparing a room."

Orna called out orders and led the way through the bailey and past the kitchens. The smell of fresh bread baking in the ovens bombarded his senses as he rushed past.

Broderick ignored the stares and whispers of the clansmen eyeing him suspiciously as he followed Orna down the familiar hall he'd run through as a young lad. The cold stone corridor stretching to the far edges of his memory.

They arrived at the room designated for the lass. The walls were the same, but the room had changed since the last time he'd been here. He could barely see the faded etchings he and his brother had scratched into the surface on those rare occasions when Ewan was allowed to just be a lad. Not the first son.

"In here. Lay her on the bed and take yer leave." Orna commanded. "I'll call for ye if needed." And with that, she pushed Broderick out the door before hurriedly closing it behind him.

MAGGIE'S EYES fluttered open and through blurry vision, she saw a woman walking beside her protector. Gray-haired and hunched over, she reminded her of the old crones in the stories her father used to tell her as a child. The woman's lips were moving but her voice seemed to be coming through water. Maggie tried to concentrate on the words and got the impression she was ordering people about. She felt herself shifting from the warmth and protection of the man's arms and laid upon a soft bed.

He was Not Diel, was her only thought as she tried to process where she was and who these people were.

The huge warrior with blond hair who'd carried her, had watched her with concern darkening his blue eyes. There was a flash of empathy in his gaze, before the crone pushed him away and Maggie immediately felt his absence as the cold air pimpled her skin.

The woman gave her a sympathetic smile and covered her with a throw. The warmth nothing compared to the warrior's hold.

She wanted to stay awake—to stay vigilant of her surroundings, and to search out the caring blond warrior. Unfortunately, her body's betrayal had her slipping back into darkness and into the unwelcoming arms of sleep.

OUTSIDE THE DOOR, standing at his full height, Broderick was taller than most of the men he'd passed. His broad shoulders made his height seem that much more intimidating. The clansmen had gathered round, murmuring to each other, but for the moment they kept their distance.

He assessed them—men, women, children. All waiting, some looking at him expectantly, others with an expression he couldn't quite identify. They held back, not one of them approached him. Most likely had no memory of him. Some of the younger clansfolk didn't know him at all, having been born after he'd left Straik all those years ago.

None of the faces struck a chord of familiarity. The same as he'd changed since he'd last set foot in Straik, so had they. People had moved away. Others had joined the clan, either by marriage or some other means.

Lord only knew what they'd been told. Mayhap Callum

had talked nothing of him. Either way, he had no control over whatever his father had or had not said about him.

He waited, unsure of what he was supposed to do. What was the appropriate protocol?

A man, looking similar in age to Broderick, stepped forward.

"My laird." He dipped his head in a quick bow, his brown hair falling forward and covering his eyes. "Welcome back to Straik. I'm sorry it took this set of circumstances to bring ye back. Yer father and brother were good men."

A low hum of agreement moved through the group.

Broderick caught the slight hitch in the man's voice when he referred to his father and brother and Broderick could tell they were both well liked amongst the clan. Good was not the descriptor he would use for either one of them, but they'd always made sure to keep the darker side of themselves hidden from the clan. Callum especially.

Ewan was young and had just followed along with whatever their father had been teaching him. He couldn't speak to his brother's demeanor as an adult, as he'd not seen him in years. But there was no denying he was favored by the clan.

"Thank ye," he said.

"To be honest, if I may?" Broderick nodded and the man continued. "There were whispers throughout the clan. We didna think ye would return. But we are thankful ye did. We worried that Duff would step in to take a place as laird."

Over Broderick's dead body. His childhood nemesis would never lead his clan.

Never.

"Aye." The others agreed and the men bowed their heads as the women dipped into curtsies.

"I will never let that happen. Again, I thank ye for the welcome. I shall reacquaint myself with Straik and speak on the clan issues at a later time." Broderick weaved his way through the gathering, dipping his chin as they acknowledged him, pleasantly surprised by the interaction.

He wandered outside for some much needed fresh air after the stuffiness of being swarmed by memories inside the castle.

Thank goodness Orna was still here. She'd always treated him well and he trusted she would give the lass the very best care she could. If anyone could save the lass, it would be Orna.

A gust of wind swept through the courtyard and Broderick looked up to the sky. Clouds were rolling back in, and judging by the heaviness in the air, it was going to rain again tonight.

He hadn't known what to expect when he arrived, but a warm welcome wasn't it. The rare missives he'd received from his father had been laced with such disrespect Broderick wondered why he had bothered to send them at all. One would think his father would have been happy he'd left, but it never appeared that way. Callum always seemed to know where Broderick was—an interesting circumstance for a man who seemed completely uninterested in what happened to his youngest son. Broderick had always assumed Alastair had a lot to do with that.

He wouldn't have been surprised if he had been met with hostility and suspicion upon his arrival. Both leader and heir to the clan had been murdered. The killers hadn't been found. He would understand if some of the clansmen might think he had something to do with their deaths.

After being away so long, Broderick hadn't expected a fanfare welcome with pennants and celebrations. He wasn't much for celebrations, so he was fine with that. And for as many issues as he and Callum had, his father was well liked by members of the clan. Even those that thought he may have focused too much on raiding and pillaging. Any actions he'd ever taken, had always been for the betterment of the clan, the expansion of their lands. Ewan, too. As such, their deaths affected their clansmen deeply.

Broderick had no interest in raids. There was no need to expand their fortunes. The MacLeod owned more than enough land and holdings. He wanted nothing more than for the clan to be safe and happy. He could only hope that there were more members of the clan that would prefer a peaceful life. It would make this road much easier.

Some people whispered to one another as he passed, interest lifting their brows, unafraid to meet his eyes. Other tight-lipped villagers eyed him skeptically as he walked past.

Mayhap his adventures and reputation as a Mercenary had preceded his arrival. Lord only knew what their reaction would be if they found out he was also a member of the Amadán.

Broderick squared his broad shoulders and kept his eyes focused ahead as he continued on. He would not waste his time worrying about whether everyone accepted him or not. Each person would have to make the decision for themselves. He prayed that one day they would realize he would fight to the death to protect his people and lands from anyone intent on doing them harm.

Outside once again, he walked toward the cemetery, a place he'd visited many times. He followed the well-beaten path up hill until it curved around a massive centuries-old pine. A few more steps and it opened to a small clearing where a stone chapel stood.

Broderick hadn't been here in years.

The gray stone facade gathered into a triangle near the top to form a slight steeple. It wasn't the smallest chapel he'd seen, but by no means the largest. Though, it had seemed much larger when he was young.

Inside, three rows of wooden pews were arranged on the

left and right, facing the altar. As a lad, he'd sat there for hours and talked to his mother, confiding in her all his fears and worries. His gaze fell to the dirty stone floor, which seemed blasphemous to him. He suspected it was a result of the recent ceremonies that were surely held for his father and brother.

On the wall behind the pulpit, positioned in a place of prominence, was a beautiful stained glass window that always managed to capture the sunlight, no matter how dreary the day.

Vivid blues, greens, yellows, and reds formed into the shape of a thistle and filtered the waning sunlight, creating a prism of color that danced along the floor.

His mother loved that window. And Callum had surely paid a hefty fee for the piece.

Broderick paused to stare at the design, willing his mind to envision the sight of his mother as she gazed upon it. But there was nothing—the memory was lost—along with so many others. He feared what he pictured now was the imaginings of his mind. A compilation of the things he could remember about her with his brain filling in the missing pieces.

He left the chapel and walked outside to stroll the graveyard. The grass had been worn away, replaced by muddy earth ground down from the steps of all the clansmen that had visited in the past few weeks.

His father's headstone was large, even bigger than the previous lairds. A testament to how well he was liked amongst the clan. Admired and respected even, judging from the size.

Broderick stood at the foot of the grave. Waiting for the proper emotions to fill his soul. He felt almost guilty that none came. The longer he stood there, the less he felt. One might call him ungrateful and, in a sense, mayhap he was. He should pay his respects to Callum, but he owed his father nothing. He'd never given Broderick anything other than life, and he attributed that mostly to his mother, since she carried him through and saw him to birth.

His mother's gravesite lay beside his father's. Elspeth's headstone was worn smooth, weathered over time, and the ground had settled in the years since she'd passed.

He knelt, placed a hand on the cold stone and said a prayer, wishing she was still here.

His next stop was Ewan's grave. His heart gave a slight tug as he stared down at the freshly turned earth. There were times in their youth when they'd been able to enjoy brotherhood. But the times grew further and further apart the older they got. Ewan had been happy to be the son their father was grooming him to be.

Even with their troubled pasts, no matter who was to blame, Broderick was never able to reconcile with his family, and now never would. For that he was regretful. The only thing he could and would do was avenge their deaths.

"I vow to ye, father," he looked toward the large headstone, the moniker bitter on his tongue, and then to his brother's, "and to ye, brother, I will find who took ye down and stole ye from yer clan. They'll pay with their lives. I swear to ye." Broderick tapped his clenched fist to his chest and turned to head back to the castle.

As he walked, he thought of the lass. How was she faring? Orna's hands were more than capable, but the lass was in such an awful state. Her bruises reminded him of the ones he'd seen on his mother. The marks left upon her by his father. No woman deserved to be treated that way. Memories of the past flooded his brain, and he pushed them away.

Broderick had been unable to help his mother. But he could help the lass.

He prayed she was strong enough to fight through her injuries.

Anger thrummed through him like a fierce storm he could barely control. The thought of what the poor lass had been through made him want to exact revenge on the bastard behind the attack.

What an amazing woman she was to have survived such an ordeal.

A true warrior.

CHAPTER 4

*E*very inch of skin and every bone in Maggie's body hurt. With what could only be the Lord's help, she'd somehow survived the night. Though the amount of pain radiating through her had her wondering if it was worth the fight.

She struggled to open her eyes, still sensitive from Diel's punches, and bright light streamed through a slotted window. Maggie moaned and her head rolled to the side, away from the light. Odd, there wasn't a window in the room where Diel kept her. She inhaled and the air smelled fresh and clean, nothing like the musky dampness she'd grown used to.

Maggie risked opening her eyes again. Her vision was a bit blurry, but she saw a vase filled with fresh-cut flowers. It added a cheeriness to the room and their scent wafted through the air, tickling her nose, but in a good way.

The bed she lay upon was piled high with thick throws, keeping her comfortably warm.

Images of a blond warrior danced on the edges of her memory. The heat of a fire in the frigid night air. Being jostled on a horse. Nay, she was no longer in Diel's keep. But where was she?

There had been an old woman, too. A healer. Where did she go?

Diel's angry face flashed before her eyes.

Maggie's pulse quickened as she thought of the possibilities. Maybe his men had found her after she'd collapsed in the woods and brought her back to her captor. What if her mind was playing tricks on her and the kind and gentle blond warrior was a figment of her imagination conjured up in a moment of utter desperation?

Don't be silly, Maggie, she thought as she blinked away the nightmare. She refused to believe he wasn't a real flesh and blood man. She remembered his heat enveloping her.

He was real, but could he be trusted or was he another one of Diel's men?

Why would he have rescued her then have a healer look after her if he only planned to continue Diel's torture? Besides, this place was unfamiliar to her.

She gulped for air to quell the sudden terror and doubt that tried to rip through her mind.

For whatever reason, Diel had let her go. She needed to accept that she had escaped him and his torment.

A shiny object drew her eyes to the nightstand by the bed. The brooch that Maggie had found in the woods lay on the wool scrap she'd found with it. She reached for it and stopped as a knife's edge pain sliced through her ribs. She breathed through it, tried again, and snatched them up. After a quick glance at the door, she hastily wrapped the brooch up in the fabric and shoved the small bundle under the covers. Her hope was that the wee piece of jewelry would aid her in learning the true identity of her tormentor.

To do that, she would need to determine where she was.

The door opened and she shifted her leg over the brooch, keeping the item her secret for now.

"Och, my lady, dinna ye fash." Maggie recognized the woman's gentle voice just before she appeared in her vision.

"I didna think ye were going to make it through the night." She was red-cheeked, round faced and when she moved across the room, she blocked the light from the window. "I'm thankful I was wrong."

The woman walked to the bed and began to reach for her.

Expecting a cruel blow, Maggie instinctively drew back.

Concern darkened the woman's eyes, and she clucked her tongue, tucking a wisp of gray hair back under her cap.

"'Tis alright, lass." The older woman gently placed a cool hand on Maggie's forehead. "I'm sorry to have frightened ye. I'm Orna."

Maggie relaxed at the kind touch. She was only trying to help her.

Her eyes darted to the weathered hand now resting on her arm, and she pulled away. The woman was being genuine, but a voice in the dark recesses of her mind reminded her to be careful. To trust no one.

She hated how Diel's treatment of her made her question everything. Kind gestures that before she would have soaked up with love before now made her look for a sinister meaning behind the action.

Orna frowned, but otherwise ignored the gesture. "Ye must be wonderin' where ye are?"

Maggie remained silent. If she was wrong about the blond warrior's rescue, and all of this was just another one of Diel's cruel jokes, she wouldn't give him the satisfaction of playing a part in it.

"Dinna ye fash, my lady, ye're safe here." She stroked Maggie's hair as she continued to speak. "I dinna know who hurt ye so, but ye have the word of the laird of Straik Castle that no further harm will come to ye."

Straik Castle. Maggie said the name over in her mind, as her gaze wandered around the room. She'd heard the name, but new naught of its laird. But one thing was certain, she was very far from home.

Diel had been so careful not to reveal his name before, so it was possible this was his castle. But if she was back under his captivity, why would he reveal it now?

The healer stood and went over to a basin set in the corner and wet a cloth. The water splashed as she twisted the cloth to squeeze out the excess water, then she returned to Maggie's bedside. With great care, she tended to the cuts on her face.

Maggie ignored the sting—compared to what she'd been through, they were nothing—and observed in silence.

"In case ye were of the curious sort, I've been the healer for Clan MacLeod for," she paused, her hand in midair, deep in thought, "well, let's just say for a verra long time." She looked down and smiled.

Clan MacLeod? Her golden warrior, her savior—was he a MacLeod? Maggie's father had spoken highly of Laird MacLeod. He'd met him over the years and had always said the laird was a kind man that put his people first.

She took note of Orna's sash, the yellow and black plaid with a hint of red.

The MacLeod plaid. Very different from the plaid she'd seen on Diel and his men.

Maggie's shoulders relaxed a bit as relief washed over her and she sunk into the pillows.

At no time would Diel hire a healer. Not to tend to her wounds, anyway. He'd once told her he liked the way the deep purple and blue bruises contrasted against her pale skin.

'It brings life to yer drab appearance,' he'd spat.

"Anyway," Orna continued, "ye'll like the laird. We've a new one." She leaned close to Maggie's ear and whispered, "He's the second son and he's just come back after years away." She shot a brief look toward the door. The new laird is the one who found ye in the woods and brought ye here. He's been in to check on ye throughout the night. He'll make sure ye're protected."

Found her in the woods? So, the warrior had *not* been a dream?

Maggie's mind was hazy, and the night before was a scrambled mess of memories. She had faint memories of a large man lifting her, of riding safely in his warm arms. Of being placed gently in this bed.

Could it be true? Was she really safe?

After her ordeal, she was having a hard time believing her mind wasn't playing tricks on her. What was real and what was a dream?

"He is dealing with his own tragedy." The woman continued. "Lost his father and brother in one fell swoop, he did." Orna looked down and gave her a warm smile. "All information ye'll find out on yer own soon enough."

Her blond warrior had suffered his own tragedy recently with losing his family members. Maggie wondered what the circumstances were surrounding their deaths. Had the MacLeod's come under attack the same way her village had?

Orna stood and walked to the basin to rinse the cloth.

"When Broderick," she paused, "though I guess I should address him properly as laird now. Anyway, when he carried ye in last night, barely a breath was escaping ye. Out there in the cold with just yer shift. Ye must've been chilled to the bone. The first thing I did was wrap ye in throws to warm ye up."

There was a gentle knock on the door and Maggie tensed.

"'Tis alright, lass." Orna patted her arm and moved over to open the door—only slightly, a mere sliver.

Maggie couldn't see who was on the other side, but she hoped they stayed there for the moment.

The old woman had talked of the MacLeod. Judging by the difference in plaids, Diel wasn't a MacLeod. A relation? Mayhap. She had no way of knowing since his given name had never been revealed during her entire time in captivity.

Orna whispered something to the person at the door then closed it with a soft *thump*.

"That was the laird himself, coming back to check on ye." Steam rose from a cup cradled in her palms and she set it on the table beside the bed. "He even hand-delivered the tisanes that will put something in yer belly and help with the pain. His concern runs deep and true."

Maggie was at a loss for words. She'd been deprived of such kindness for so long she wasn't sure how to react. Diel could not be the laird Orna spoke about—he was void of benevolence and compassion. One couldn't be so cruel and mask those traits so well that his clansmen found him to be kind and caring.

She had never seen any of the castle folk in the time she was being held by Diel. What she'd seen of his castle had been dark and damp. Foreboding fairly oozed from every stone, every crevice, every tattered tapestry. It was nothing like the bright and cheerful room she currently found herself in.

She allowed herself to relax just a bit. Secure in the knowledge this wasn't Diel's castle. "That is verra kind of him." Maggie's throat was dry and her voice hoarse from screaming into the cold night air.

"Do ye think yer stomach can handle some sustenance?" Orna smiled.

"I think so." Maggie nodded.

"Let's get you sat up a wee bit." With a gentle hand Orna helped her to a sitting position.

Pain pierced Maggie's side as she choked back an agonized cry.

Those last kicks Diel had rained upon her before sending her off with his men were still fresh. Paired that with all the running she'd done and the ride with her savior on the horse —Laird MacLeod—any type of movement shot like fire through her body.

"I'm sorry, lass." Orna took the mug and held it up to her dry, cracked lips. "Here, but go slowly."

Maggie carefully placed her battered lips to the brim for a tentative sip. The liquid was bitter on her tongue, and she couldn't help but make a face at the unpleasant taste. Doubt and suspicion continued to creep through her mind. For all she knew, it could be a poisoned broth. She might have laughed if she thought it wouldn't cause her great pain. Even still, the warm liquid soothed as it flowed down her throat.

"Aye, 'tis no' the best drink ye've e'er had, but ye'll thank me when yer pain starts to ebb away." Orna's kindness twinkled in her eyes.

In her few lucid moments during the journey here, she'd instinctively felt safe and warm wrapped in the strong arms of Laird MacLeod. Maggie ascertained Diel was playing no part in the current happenings.

After a few more sips, Orna took the cup away and placed it on the table. "Okay, let's get ye settled back down."

"I'd rather stay sitting, if ye dinna mind?" Her voice was slightly stronger. She needed to view her surroundings instead of lying down and staring up at the ceiling.

"Och, ye're a feisty one." Orna laughed. "That's good. Ye keep that fighting spirit and ye'll come through just fine. Ye can stay sitting up, but the broth should make ye a wee bit sleepy. If ye start to feel woozy just lay back. Dinna want ye falling out of the bed."

Maggie started to smile and sucked in a breath when her lips threatened to crack further, and she just bobbed her head up and down.

"Of course!" Orna exclaimed. "Yer poor lips. I have some salve that will help with that. Ye poor thing. Let me go fetch it and I'll be back soon."

Orna left, pulling the door shut behind her. Maggie scoured the room with her eyes, memorizing everything, looking for clues. If she was lucky, she might find something she could use as a weapon if the need arises.

The accommodations were tiny but clean, bright and warm. Her gaze fell upon the delicately carved basin stand in the corner. It appeared to be made from the same wood as the bed and had been sanded to a smooth finish. The small chamber was much more ornate and grander than the small croft that she'd lived in her whole life. She imagined this room was for a tot, though the absence of any real decorations would make it a bit somber for a child. It was a far cry from the frigid, barren room with the icy stone floor she'd slept on at Diel's castle.

Fresh air blew in through the open window and she was thrilled to see a slice of sky once again. She closed her eyes and, as deep as her pained chest would allow, drew in a slow deep breath of chilly air. The scent of spruce and peat smoke, mixed with the fragrance of the flowers set out on the table.

Diel had tried to take everything from her and failed. She was still alive, thanks to a total stranger who had come to her rescue. He'd housed her in this small guest room out of the kindness of his heart. Or was there some other reason? Did he know what had happened to her village?

This was the closest thing to freedom she'd felt in weeks, and it sparked a glimmer of hope—which terrified her even further. Hope was something she couldn't fully embrace, not yet.

A weapon, she silently reminded herself, and resumed her search.

She yawned, and her lips began to bleed anew. Orna had been truthful when she'd said the broth would make Maggie tired. It felt as if a warm blanket cushioned her weary bones. The pain was still there but was less noticeable. She struggled to keep her eyes open, to keep her wits about her, and to savor her current peace of mind for as long as possible. In sleep, she was vulnerable and couldn't protect herself. Yet her body needed to heal so she *could* protect herself in the future.

Maggie embraced the feeling of the pain slowly ebbing away bit by wee bit and soon, the pull of sleep was too much. Her eyes closed and she drifted off to a restful sleep. Her first in far too long.

IN THE GREAT HALL, Broderick paused and took in the large room. Long and rectangular, its ceiling rose to the open wooden beam rafters. Heavy tapestries hung on the walls, each one depicting a scene his father deemed important, their muted colors and tattered edges showing their age. One embroidered cloth showing a boar hunt drew his attention. He paused, studying the scene. How ironic that his father had died doing the thing he loved. If only it was the actual hunt that had killed him and Ewan.

To be ambushed on their own lands during a hunt when all the men were focusing on their prey was a coward's way to eliminate one's enemy. Broderick would avenge the deaths of his father and brother. But he had to suss out the killer first.

The wooden dais stood centered at the far wall. Behind it,

swords of former lairds hung in tribute. The long table was vacant of all utensils and food. The ornate chair that only the laird could sit upon was draped in the clan plaid with Callum's own claymore laid across the arms. An honor to his late father.

The gesture humbled Broderick, and it reminded him how much the clan respected tradition. The same thing had been done for each passing laird. It also showed him how much the clan respected his father. Broderick still had trouble separating Callum, the caring Laird MacLeod, from Callum, the uncaring, cruel father he'd known as a lad.

"Ye came." Alastair Lewis's familiar voice broke into his thoughts.

Broderick turned to see his Amadán mentor, the one person who'd always treated him like he belonged. Alastair had noticed his potential when he was young and showed him a world he could be a part of.

A tall, lanky man, he had a tinge of gray hair at his temples and a slight, barely discernible limp. That said, Alastair was not one to underestimate. Broderick had seen the man's strength with his own eyes and been personally trained by Alastair to become the warrior that he was today.

"I knew ye would. We have much to discuss."

Broderick reached out to clasp his hand in a vigorous shake.

"My laird." Alastair stopped in front of Broderick and swept his hand away. Instead, he enveloped him in a powerful hug.

Broderick's throat knotted with unshed emotions for the man who'd been more like a father to him than Callum.

"Alastair, please." They broke their embrace and he stepped back. "My laird, my arse."

The last time they had seen each other was a month ago,

just before Broderick had left on his latest mission in Inverness. The one he'd been called back from.

"Protocol must be followed." Alastair said. "Ye're the leader of our clan now."

"No' by my choice." He shook his head, turned and glanced around the hall.

The men gathered there sized him up as the women huddled together, whispering behind their hands. He understood their curiosity and accepted that he would be the topic of conversation for some time. He would prove his ability to lead them, and to right the wrongs shed upon them with the deaths of Callum and Ewan.

"The clansfolk's reaction was more than I expected." Broderick lowered his voice for Alastair's ears only. "Kinder," he mumbled.

They hadn't outright told him to leave, which was something that Broderick had fully anticipated. He'd detected almost a sense of relief at his return, which spoke volumes to Duff's acceptance within the clan. Mayhap this had been his destiny all along. Change, though not always welcome, was oft times a good thing.

"They'll accept ye, just fine." Alastair clapped him on the back. "Ye'll make a strong leader."

He couldn't hold back the laugh that erupted from deep within his chest.

"Ye know as well as I that I'm no' cut out for this life. Naught I've done up until this point shows that."

"Nay," Alastair shook his head. "'Tis no' true. Ye've led many a team of men on many dangerous missions. Ye've recruited new members into the Amadán. Strong, trustworthy brothers."

"A team of men. No' a whole clan. I wasna responsible for their livelihood. Their households and families." So much responsibility. "This is clearly no' the same situation."

"I ken 'tis no' what ye expected. But there are times when the fates have a different plan for us." Alastair spoke with his usual wisdom.

Broderick chuckled and gazed at the man that had served the place of father to him more than his own blood. The one person he looked up to as a lad when his own father had turned his back on him. Over the years, Alastair had shown Broderick what it was like to truly lead from a position of respect that was earned and not demanded. That was the difference between Alastair and Callum. He was fully aware that the Callum he and his mother knew was far different than the Callum the clan knew.

Broderick would do all he could to live up to Alastair's high expectations.

"Who's the lass?" Alastair asked.

He'd been wondering when he would ask about her.

"I dinna know." Broderick's big shoulders lifted and fell. "I found her in the woods last night, a ways from MacLeod lands." Anger lanced his chest, and he clenched his fists. "She was attacked, Alastair. Savagely. Mistreated for who knows how long. Judging by her wounds, mayhap weeks."

"That is horrific and inexcusable." Alastair shook his head and placed a comforting hand on Broderick's shoulder.

"Aye, 'tis. Ye know I canna let it pass." He dipped his head and spoke quietly. "Whether 'tis the Amadán or me alone, I will find whoever is responsible for the injuries done to the lass."

"I'd expect naught less from ye." Alastair swept his arm out. "Come, let us sit. Ye can tell me how ye came to find her."

Broderick followed his mentor to the hearth where two large wooden chairs faced the fire. Since it was still mid-day, flames burned strong, licking up the insides of the stone hearth, their warm glow dancing along the floor and heating his skin. Again, he waited for sadness to overcome him—the usual emotion one felt when one lost his remaining family. And still, naught came.

Alastair sat, grunting as he did so.

"My laird." A young lad—the red-headed boy who'd fetched Orna—hurried over and dipped his head in a slight bow.

Alastair cleared his throat, reminding Broderick that the boy was talking to him.

I am laird now.

These people were now his duty, his responsibility. Not his father's nor his brother's.

The weight of everything that had occurred bore down on his shoulders. 'Twas a heavy burden for him to carry. He wasn't convinced he could succeed in being the leader that these people needed.

"Would be like me to see to yer horse now, sir?" The lad had freckles dotting his pale cheeks and the bridge of his nose and couldn't be more than ten summers.

With everything that happened since he'd arrived, he had forgotten he'd left Goliath alone in the courtyard. The beast wouldn't forgive him and would make sure he knew it the next time Broderick was in his presence.

"Aye. Give him a good rub down and lots of snacks." He reached into his pocket and pulled out a silver coin and tossed it to the lad.

"Aye, sir!" He smiled and his green eyes widened as he stared at the coin. "I'll treat him most kindly. Ye have my word."

At least he was all right with the younger ones. Perhaps he would get lucky and the others would be just as easy.

Broderick took a seat and watched the lad run out of the hall, having tucked the coin safely away. He and Alastair sat, stoic, embers shoot into the air as the wood cracked and settled.

"Let us drink," Broderick declared, knowing the older man would take him up on his offer.

Alastair wasn't one to turn down an offer of fine ale.

He lifted his hand to flag down a serving wench walking nearby. Like the lad, she hustled over to them.

"Bring us the finest ale Straik has and a cup for each of us." He dipped his head in Alastair's direction.

"Aye, sir." The wench nodded once and scurried off to heed his request.

"'Twill be nice if the castle folk accept me as their laird." While he could get used to having servants at his beck and call, he didn't want them to think he was completely incapable of doing things for himself.

"Aye," Alastair agreed. "Ye need to give them time. Lest ye forget, yer father was well respected and admired, and they've been under his leadership for years. I ken he was two different men when it came to his clan and his family."

"Truer words have never been spoken." Broderick nodded. "I dinna understand. Was he like that before my mother? Brutish to those he claimed to love."

"Yer mother." Alastair sighed. "She was much too sweet of a lass to be tied to yer father. 'Twas no' her choice, but alliances being as such, she had no say in the matter."

"I think of her often." Broderick swallowed the lump lodged in his throat at the memory of his mother.

"As ye should. She loved ye verra much. But ye're here now." Alastair stated, changing the subject.

Here. At Straik.

The thought of being planted in the same place was unappealing. He was used to his freedom. Free from the burdens of a clan.

Alastair was well aware of his feelings on the matter, but

it was more important that the clan not fall into the hands of Duff. As unconventional as the transfer of leadership from Callum to Duff would've been, it would've made sense in this case. After all, Broderick had sworn off Straik and any claim he had to it long ago. But hell would freeze over before Duff ever led the MacLeod clan. They were honest, hard-working people, and Duff was shite.

No matter what oath he had sworn to himself about never returning to Straik, everything had changed with the deaths of Callum and Ewan. Broderick would never subject his people to that bastard's idea of lairdship.

"Do ye think the lass is a MacDonald?" Alastair pulled Broderick out of his memories with the mention of their neighboring clan.

Duff was a MacDonald but was no reflection of his clan. Even if they and the MacLeod had had their fair share of disagreements in the past, for the most part they were good people.

"I dinna ken." He thought of the injured lass currently being tended by Orna. "Mayhap. I found her on their lands."

If she were a MacDonald, would she want to stay at Straik? Did he want her to?

The serving wench set two cups of ale on the small wooden table and left them.

He lifted his in a toast. Slàinte mhath." *Good health.*

Broderick took a long swallow of the ale, the taste lighter than he preferred. Mayhap he should switch to whisky.

For a long moment, the two men sat in silence in front of the roaring fire, drinking the ale that was refilled as soon as their cups were empty. They shared an understanding in the silence between them and no words needed to be spoken.

"Ye canna save everyone, Broderick." Alastair seemed to know what Broderick was thinking about.

The lass.

"But I can try." He nodded and gave him a wry smile.

He couldn't keep her out of his thoughts—her bruised, battered body continually flashed in his mind. What horrors had she suffered? The lass was a warrior to have survived. He could relate to that and admired her for it. She deserved respect. Honor. And he'd be sure she saw those from him.

A log settled and sparks crackled as they shot into the air. Broderick watched the embers as they floated up before burning out.

"So, ye've really naught idea who the lass is?" Alastair finally broke the silence.

Broderick shook his head, then smoothed back the blond hairs that fell into his face with a swipe of his hand.

"I'd just settled down for the night and thought I heard a female voice curse. Yes, when I found her, she could do naught more than groan. So, I couldna have heard her." He took a long pull of ale and rested the cup on the arm of the chair. "E'en now, I fear I may be going daft. 'Tis truly a miracle I found her."

"Sometimes, the world has an odd way of making things appear."

Broderick huffed. "Dinna ye start with yer fairy notions, old man. Ye ken I dinna believe in that."

"I'm only suggesting that since the lass canna speak, something had to alert ye to the girl." He rapped his knuckles on the wooden arm of the chair, tapping out a melody. "How did she get in the woods, I wonder?"

"I dinna ken. There are no villages anywhere near where I found her. With her injuries, she couldna have traveled far. Mayhap she was abandoned. I dinna know."

Once again, anger rose in his chest. Men who treated women like animals didn't deserve to be walking on this earth. Breathing the same air. He would find the man responsible, and he would have his head.

"Otherwoldly help or naught, I found her just in time." Broderick brushed his hand down his thigh. "I fear she would have died if I hadna found her when I did."

"Ye're a good man, Broderick. Ye'll make a fine laird."

"I dinna ken about that." Broderick frowned and shook his head.

"Ye saved the lass. As of this verra time, she breathes only because of yer actions." Alastair laid a strong hand on Broderick's shoulder, squeezing it in a comforting gesture. "I've no doubt of yer capabilities to lead. Ye're strong. Ye've proven that o'er and o'er. Ye care about others. That in itself will make ye a better leader than yer father and brother could e'er be."

Broderick may be a brute as far as his job went, but not when it came to women. He'd never hurt them. Not on purpose anyway.

He thought of his mother, Elspeth. Callum MacLeod hadn't wanted to look at his youngest son was because he saw his wife's face in Broderick's. He shook off the memory that lingered at the edge of his mind whenever he thought of his dear mother.

"Get up." Alastair took a last sip of ale, pushed up from his chair, and arched his back to stretch. "Sitting is doing us no good."

Broderick set his mug on the table near his chair and stood.

"Someone should have conveyed that information to my father." He followed Alastair out of the Great Hall and a cynical laugh slipped past his lips. "Maybe then he wouldna have beat me to near death that night."

His back still held the scars of that thrashing. The rough ridges a constant reminder that his father blamed him for his mother's death.

"Where are we going?" he asked.

Alastair ignored him and continued outside to the court-yard, around the well, and down the steps toward the sea gate.

"Yer mother fell and injured herself, Broderick. Despite what yer father said, 'twas not yer fault the sharp wood pierced her gut and festered. Even Orna couldna save her."

"I ken that. Now. No' so much when I was a lad." His father hadn't cared that he was just a child with no knowl-edge of the healing ways. His accusations had rooted them-selves deep within Broderick's mind.

"What I endured at his hand that night was naught compared to what my mother had to go through as his wife." With every lash of the switch against his flesh inflicted upon him by his father that night, Broderick realized how strong his mother truly way, considering all Callum had done to her.

"Mother hated that father was training Ewan to be a monster like him. Unfortunately, she'd been powerless to keep it from happening.

After her death, in Callum's twisted mind, his youngest son had been a reminder of why his wife no longer walked the earth. Not because he'd especially cared for her—he did not. But because she had borne him Ewan, who had proved to be everything in a son that a father could have ever wanted in a son. That was the only reason she'd held even a sliver of the elder MacLeod's respect. Not that it had been enough to stop him from raising his hand to her. Which was often and usually for no reason.

Broderick remembered many days she would emerge from their bedchambers with bruises marring her otherwise pale skin. Much like the bruises on the lass's face, arms, and legs. Each time, she'd given him a small, forced smile and held a delicate finger to her lips to keep him from protesting.

As he'd looked into her sad, defeated eyes, he'd vowed never to lay a hand on a woman.

He'd kept that promise. To this day, he loved his mother so and missed her dearly.

Broderick's thoughts were interrupted by the sound of his mentor's boots on the stone steps. He shook his head to clear out the sad memories from his past. That wasn't his life anymore. His father no longer had sway over him.

They navigated the steps to a tunnel that opened onto a beach littered with rocks rounded by eons of water brushing over them. The fresh and salty sea air was a scent he associated with happier times during his childhood. The sound of the water lapping and rippling over the rocky shore a welcome melody to Broderick's ears and helped clear away the last remnants of painful memories.

"What are yer thoughts on who attacked Callum and Ewan?" Broderick valued Alastair's opinion.

"If I had to dare a guess, I'd say the MacDonald." Alastair's answer seemed uncertain. "He's been wreaking havoc in the area and 'tis no secret he and yer father no longer considered each other allies."

"Ye really think he'd attack the clan that raised his son?" Broderick caught himself when his boot slipped on the loose, slimy rocks.

"I dinna ken. From what I've been told, MacDonald is in failing health as of late. 'Tis possible he wanted to make one last attempt at a land grab, futile as that would be. Or mayhap he has someone in his ear." Alastair paused and faced the water, looking far out to the horizon.

"He's never forgiven yer father for raising Duff as a MacLeod." Alastair stared off into the direction of the Outer Hebrides, no doubt thinking of his own past and longing for loved ones long gone. His mentor had also experienced great loss.

"I thought that was done as a deal between the two of them?" His father never shared anything with him. The reason for Duff's presence in their lives had been no different.

"Aye, but when Duff became of age, ye recall he was supposed to return to his own clan. He didna, and instead stayed with yer da."

"He should have gone back to his own clan and led them as he wanted," Broderick mumbled. It had always irked him that Duff had stayed.

"Nay." Alastair clucked his tongue. "His father wouldna allow him to lead the MacDonald with a hard hand, as he'd wanted to."

The bastard. The revelation didn't surprise Broderick at all.

"It still doesna make any sense to me that the MacDonald would plan and execute a plan to murder Callum and Ewan. It seems completely outside of the old man's character."

"I tend to agree with ye," Alastair nodded, "but I dinna know of anyone else that would attempt such a plan."

"I think there is something amiss that we havena discovered yet."

Broderick sighed, ran a hand through his hair, and watched the waves rolling onto the shore.

"Ye may be right," Alastair said. "I've no doubt ye will be the one to uncover the truth."

"Do ye have any proof that 'twas the MacDonald or just a feeling?"

"Nay, nothing more than my gut telling me 'tis so."

"Ye've searched the area of the attack?" Broderick asked, already knowing the answer.

"Aye. More than once." Alastair sighed and pinched the bridge of his crooked nose. "We found naught in the woods that would lead us to the attacker."

Danger always played a large part in a boar hunt. Being ambushed by an unseen enemy on one's own land was different altogether. His father and brother had been taken completely unawares. A factor hunters rarely considered or planned for.

"I'd like to search the area myself." Broderick bent over, grabbed a rock, and tossed it into the water.

"Of course." Alastair turned to him. "We can ride to the area whenever ye are ready."

"Was there anyone else that may have wanted to cause the MacLeod harm? What of the MacKinnon?" Broderick asked about one of their nearest neighbors.

"Nay." Alastair shook his head before continuing on along the shore, ignoring the water wetting his boots. "Callum recently raided some of the villages on MacKinnon land, but there have been no signs of retaliation. The MacDonald is the only person that I could think of that would be foolish enough to kill our laird and his heir. He is no' known for acting before thinking, but he's older now and rumors are circling that his mind is weakening. Which, again, leads me to believe he has someone in his ear, swaying him. And if he's too far from sanity he wouldna be thinking about what the circumstances may mean for the overall stability of his own clan. Mayhap they have some clansmen whose bloodlust is strong."

"I've dealt with many men of that ilk." Broderick nodded. "We both have. They usually dinna act so strong and brave when they have to face a foe head on. 'Tis no greater satisfaction than making them pay for their actions."

This far from the castle, the sounds of daily life were a dull hum drowned out by the constant push and pull of the waves. He sighed, unhappy with the circumstances he found himself in. This was not the direction in which he'd foreseen his life heading in.

He was a mercenary, for Christ's sake. A man for hire. If someone needed something or someone recovered, Broderick MacLeod was their man. He wasn't meant to be kept in one place. Yet, here he was—his family gone, laird of a castle, and leader of a clan he'd had no connection to for years. Circumstances beyond his control had now forced him to accept a life he never wanted.

"Have ye sent anyone out to see if they can find out information?" Broderick asked.

"Aye," Alastair nodded, rubbing his stubbled chin. "We've a few men dispersed."

If Broderick discovered the MacDonald was the one responsible for him being called home and losing his freedom—whether the old man was already near death or no'—he would avenge his father's name and mete out the necessary justice. In doing so, he would restore his clan's legacy with honor and integrity, not disgrace and mayhem.

One way or another, Broderick would restore peace to MacLeod lands.

"Do ye think there's a chance the attack and the lass could be connected?" Broderick asked.

"Hard to know." Alastair tugged his earlobe. "Mayhap."

"Where's Duff?" Broderick inquired, though he really cared naught. The last person he wanted to see was the one who took Broderick's place in his own father's eyes.

"Yer da had sent him on a mission a fortnight before his death."

"What mission and why did ye no' call him back?" Broderick raised a brow in question. "Surely, 'tis what my father would have wanted."

"Ye ken yer da was no' happy unless he was trying to expand the boundaries of MacLeod lands." Alastair turned to head back to Straik. "And Duff was none the happier to terrorize a village of lesser might. That's what he was doing, following yer father's orders."

"How my father chose Duff over me, I'll never understand." Broderick spoke through clenched teeth and shook his head in disbelief. "Nor, how Duff has been able to hide his true self from everyone. For someone to take such pleasure in other's misery and revel in it," he blew out an exasperated breath. "I hope I never learn that thirst. I take pride in the work I do, but 'tis for justice. 'Tis no' for sport."

"Ye're a good man, Broderick. 'Tis why I sent for ye first." He glanced up at a gull crying overhead. "I called Duff back as well, but Straik needs a genuine leader. Someone that will bring glory back to the MacLeod name. The clan needs ye."

"I vow to try my best. It willna be easy. Especially if the clan was happy under my father's type of leadership."

"Look around ye, at yer people. Ye can see they're accepting of ye. They may fash a bit as they dinna ken ye. But 'tis been a long time since ye've been home." He continued, "No' everyone was happy with the idea of Duff becoming laird. Selfishness and cruelty are no' the traits everyone wants from their leader. He may have hidden the most unbearable traits of himself, but those were always prevalent. I believe ye'll find ye have more allies than ye think."

Broderick gave Alastair a curt nod. "When do ye expect Duff back?"

"I may have waited much longer to send word out to him than I did ye." His mentor smiled, a twinkle in his wise eyes. "Guess ye can call me selfish in that respect. But, alas, I did reach out and he and his men should arrive within a sennight. I expect he willna be happy to see ye here."

"Understood." Broderick chuckled. "I'm sure he'll be quite surprised when he arrives, considering he probably already thinks he's laird."

"Aye, I expect so."

"I want to check on the lass." Orna said she was resting somewhat comfortably, but what if she'd regressed? "When I'm done, I'd like to ride out to where the attack took place."

"Come find me. We can ride out together."

"I'll get to the bottom of this. When I do, the flash of my blade will be the last thing he sees."

Alastair stretched his arms out, cracking his back.

"Let us get back." He placed a hand on Broderick's shoulder. "Welcome home, son."

Son. This wasn't the first time his mentor had called him that. The word usually sounded foreign to Broderick's ears. But the combination of being home—here at Straik—and hearing it from a man he respected and who meant so much to him, gave the word new meaning. He was struck by the realization that, after all the years he had stayed away, he'd come to miss the place he used to call home.

He ignored Alastair's laugh and hurried his pace to take the steps two at a time.

It was past time he checked in on the lass.

CHAPTER 5

*M*aggie didn't know how long she'd been asleep when a knock sounded and Orna poked her gray head in.

"Can I come in, my lady?"

Maggie was still a bit groggy but couldn't help but noticing that Orna didn't have to unlock the door before she entered. Another hint showing that this wasn't Diel's keep. He'd never leave her in an unlocked room.

Orna opened the door the rest of the way and stepped into the room—but she wasn't alone. The man standing behind Orna filled the space of the doorway and Maggie understandably watched him warily, though his expression looked more worried than angered.

"I came in earlier, but ye were sleeping so soundly, I just let ye be." Orna shifted her gaze from Maggie to the large warrior, tracking the direction of Maggie's gaze, which was fixed on the man standing behind her, and she sighed. "Och, dinna fash, my lady. This is Laird MacLeod. He found ye in the woods, remember?"

He didn't come into the room any further. Just watched

from afar with his brow creased, as his gaze slid from one of her injuries to the next. Part of her squirmed at the scrutiny, but the other part of her sat up straighter, jutting her chin as far forward as she could without hurting.

Laird MacLeod grinned in reaction. He was vaguely familiar. But just barely. His features, even with is strong jaw and build, exuded strength, but not in a brutal way. Just one look at Diel and you knew he was evil. This man was just the opposite. There was warmth in his blue eyes.

The faint memories she had of their night ride, of his warm arms wrapped around her tickled at the edge of her mind. If she heard his voice, her memories may click into place. But she didn't dare ask him to speak for fear of making a fool of herself.

Orna looked back to Laird MacLeod and addressed him. "Have a care, milliard. Ye dinna want to alarm to the lass."

"Aye. 'Tis not my intent."

That voice. The deep burr danced across her memory, and she let her squared shoulders drop, feeling more relaxed.

"How are ye feeling, lass?" His deep timber was cloaked in kindness.

"Better. Thank ye," Maggie answered with bated breath. She eyed the chair beside the window. Rays of golden sun fell on the seat. She wanted nothing more than to feel the sun heating her skin.

The laird studied her and followed her gaze. "Do ye want to sit in the chair?"

"I would like that verra much."

Orna came near. "Weel, let's get ye in it, then. My laird, avert yer eyes, please."

"Thank ye," Maggie whispered. The woman commanding the laird to turn so she could have her privacy was so thoughtful.

Laird MacLeod faced the opposite wall, and she got a

view of his massive shoulders and muscular back. Despite his massive size and obvious strength, he came off as tender and caring.

She was thankful that he turned around without a second thought and offered no fight. Plenty of men would have refused to afford her the privacy from their prying eyes.

"Here," Orna lifted the throw and folded it down toward the foot of the bed. "Now, no fast movements. Actually," she paused and walked over to the chair and pushed it closer to the bed, its legs scraping along the stone floor. "Yer feet were badly cut from running barefoot in the forest. I fear if ye step on them yer pain will come back anew."

Maggie carefully slid her legs over the side of the bed and with Orna's help, she managed to sit in the chair without putting too much of her weight on her feet.

Orna looked to the door and called for the MacLeod. "My laird, yer assistance now, please." She grabbed a throw and covered Maggie's legs with the cloth, shielding them from the man's eyes. "'Tis okay, my lady. The laird means ye no harm. He's quite nice," she whispered before moving to one side of the chair to allow him access to the other.

Maggie studied him closely as he came near. His chiseled jaw, his blond hair, his blue eyes, dark with concern. He was so very different from Diel. He was very polite and careful not to make any contact with her as, together, he and Orna cautiously maneuvered the chair to its original place beside the window. His arms, corded with muscle—those same strong arms that kept her warm the night he'd found her— doing most of the lifting. Maggie got the feeling he was allowing Orna to 'assist' though he could have easily moved her himself.

Before moving back to the door, he gave her a small smile that was warmer than the throw covering her legs. Sincerity ebbed from the laird in waves and Maggie reveled in the kindness he was showing her.

The laird assumed the stance he had before Orna had called him over to assist with the chair. This time though, he was facing Maggie.

"People are curious about the mysterious woman we've got staying with us. But not to worry. Ye dinna have to see anyone until ye are ready and feel like it. Except Laird MacLeod and he will go away if ye want." Orna dipped her head in his direction near the door and gave her a wink. "He was verra anxious to know how ye fared. Here," Orna held out a small pot for Maggie to take. "It's the salve for yer lips. Rub this on them and the cracking should heal."

"Thank ye." Tears sprouted in Maggie's eyes. This stranger was showing her such kindness and seemingly without an ulterior motive. It was so different from how she'd spent the last sennight of her life.

"Of course, my lady. No need to thank me. I'm happy to do it."

After what she'd been through with Diel, Maggie should be frightened, sitting so close to a man she knew nothing about, but she wasn't. Even with his hulking size, nothing but compassion flowed from him. Her mind and her feelings contradicted themselves. Perhaps it would be more prudent to be wary of him. But there was something about Laird MacLeod that screamed safety. And Maggie knew from past experience that there were good people in the world, not only evil. She was befuddled to say the least.

The sun warming Maggie's skin felt divine, and she turned her face to the window, relishing the sensation and the sense of freedom it granted her.

Diel had kept her in a windowless room near the dungeon, deep in the belly of his castle. She hadn't seen the sun until she'd been released and now, here she was soaking in it, a free woman.

She no longer believed that this was some cruel trick Diel was playing on her, laughing at her as though she were stupid. Nay, Laird MacLeod had nothing to do with Diel. And while her safety seemed definite, she couldn't really know what his intentions were. Would she have the liberty to move about? To leave when she chose? Because she couldn't stay. One way or another she would track Diel down.

Orna walked to Maggie's bed and made a face.

Maggie followed her eyes and looked at the linens, dirtied in some spots with her blood. She felt bad. They would have to scrub to get the stains out of the cloth. A chore she used to do when she helped her mother, and not an easy task. She used to hate wash days, but what she wouldn't give to be standing beside her mother once again laundering the linens while her father was selling his wares. So much had changed so fast.

She studied the laird. Standing there silently, he crossed his strong arms. His eyes were fixed upon the stained sheets. She couldn't hide the wash of embarrassment that flooded over her. The last thing she wanted to do was cause them more work. Surely, they were already busy enough without having the extra burden of caring for her.

His brow was furrowed. Was he angry at her because of the soiled bedding? Maggie drew her bottom lip into her mouth and bit it with her teeth, ignoring the pain. She shouldn't be here causing problems and upsetting the laird.

He dragged his eyes from the bed and focused them on Maggie and his expression immediately softened and he gave her a small smile. The tiny gesture eased her distress a bit.

"Since ye are out of bed for now, how about we change

the linens? Get some laundered ones on there for ye?" Orna asked.

She gave a slight nod. "I'm verra sorry for messing the linens. I can help change them."

"Dinna apologize, lass, for things that are beyond yer control." The laird spoke in a gentle tone, his deep burr comforting. He leaned against the doorframe and crossed his legs at the ankles.

"I'll need to bring in a couple of lasses to do so. Is that all right with ye?"

Maggie nodded again and Orna gave her a sympathetic smile. "Here, let's get ye covered up. We wouldna want ye to catch a chill."

Soon, her shoulders were covered in a thick shawl and Maggie clasped it in her hands, drawing it around so the ends met at her throat.

Maggie thanked the woman with a small smile. She understood the woman's meaning. The room was quite warm. The fire had been at a full roar since she'd first awakened. She was offering the shawl as a much-needed shield.

A protection from any prying eyes of the castle folk and the watchful eyes of the laird, though he was being very respectful of her, she was still weary. And she still didn't know him, or his clan well.

There were a few things she did know though.

Aye, it was true that he'd saved her in the woods. Kept her warm through the night and the ride to Straik in the rain. He was kind and caring. And everything he'd shown her thus far told her he was a very compassionate man. The way his eyes softened every time he looked at her convinced her he wasn't cruel.

Maggie almost shed a tear at the kindness being freely given to her. She hadn't done anything to deserve it.

"We need to get some nourishment into ye, lass," Laird

MacLeod stated, his voice soft. "Ye are naught but skin and bones. Orna will get ye a hearty meal soon if ye feel ye can keep it in yer belly."

Maggie's cheeks heated and she looked away. She didn't want him to see the tears that threatened to spill. After what she'd been through recently, the smallest acts of kindness seemed to bring her to the verge of tears. Diel would just laugh at her and then slap the tears away.

"Thank ye," Maggie said quietly.

Laird MacLeod stepped aside and Orna leaned out of the doorway and waved her hands. Soon, two young women appeared, both carrying clean linens in their arms.

They entered the room, and each bowed in front of the laird and then greeted Maggie. "My lady."

Maggie didn't have the heart to tell them she was no lady. They would all find out soon enough.

She and her parents were just merchants in her former village. There was nothing noble about them. But they were hard-working. Her father had sold herbs and mushrooms that they foraged from the forest. They didn't make a lot of money, but it was enough to keep them on their land and in their small cottage. When her parent's passed, she tried to do the same thing, but times were tough. And even though she felt safe in her village, living alone wasn't easy.

Maggie watched as the maids worked together to quickly strip the bed and replace the soiled linens with fresh, clean ones.

The small, cloth package she'd tucked into the folds of the bedding fell to the floor and Maggie's eyes widened. There was no avoiding them seeing what she was hiding now.

One of the maids picked it up and studied it. "Is this yers, my lady?" she asked.

Maggie's eyes darted from the cloth-covered brooch to the laird. He watched her closely but remained silent. "Aye."

The maid smiled and handed it over to Maggie, then went about finishing making the bed.

Maggie sighed in relief as she clasped the package to her chest. No one had seen what lay inside. Well, someone had since they'd placed it on the table beside her bed. She figured that was most likely Orna's doing. They didn't question her on it further and she hoped they would soon forget that she had it. The brooch was her secret for now. Her only means to identify Diel. And the key to her revenge. The beginning step in which he'd pay for all the carnage he and his men were responsible for. Her innocence. Never before had she wished death upon someone.

Diel had changed that.

The laird made no move to take the package from her. He didn't even ask her about it. Diel would have never allowed her to keep something from him. He would have grabbed the small square right out of her hands and unwrapped it as soon as he saw it.

That was how she knew she was no longer under Diel's cruel thumb.

Freedom. Choice. Respect.

In the short time she'd been here, Maggie was given all of those. She didn't know how she would ever repay them.

Outside the door, Maggie could hear the life of the castle continuing on in their blessed innocence. All the sounds were welcome after the barren quietness of Diel's fortress.

His castle was always quiet. In all the time Maggie was there, she'd never heard or seen another woman or any children. It was as if just he and his men occupied the space. Perhaps he'd ravaged all of them too.

"Would ye like a bath, my lady? We can bring in a basin and get ye comfortable. And we'll get ye some new clothes."

A bath sounded lovely. Heavenly even. It had been so long she'd been afforded the luxury. Even before she was taken, a bath was rare. It was easier to bathe in the cool water of the loch. But she didn't want to bathe in a room full of people. "Alone?"

Orna cocked her head to the side, concern furrowing her gray brows. "If ye wish it, lass. Though, I offer assistance myself if needed."

Her shoulders relaxed and the look on Maggie's face must have said it all.

Orna smiled. "Ye hold tight, my lady. We'll be right back." She pushed the laird out in front of her, and the man didn't even hesitate. Orna started to close the door, but then stopped and gave Maggie a searching look. "Do ye want me to leave it open?"

Maggie thought for a moment. She was enjoying hearing the sounds and she didn't want to shut them out after the silence she'd been subjected to under captivity. But the thought that anyone could enter the room while Orna was gone unsettled her.

"I'll tell ye what. I'll close it for now, and when I come back, we can leave it open for a bit. How's that?"

"Thank ye," Maggie said quietly.

Orna grinned and closed the door behind her.

Wee steps, Maggie thought. Orna understood and she was grateful for the kindness being shown to her by people she hadn't known for but a day. Though she must still stay vigilant, for she didn't know who else lurked in the castle. Mayhap as the days passed, her trust would grow.

Laird MacLeod was most intriguing. She found his quiet resonance comforting in a way that surprised her.

It was as if she could trust him, and she didn't know why. Aye, he found her and brought her to safety. Was ensuring she was being well tended to. His kindness reached far in helping her assess him as a man. Even his hovering near the door didn't put her on edge. It almost felt like he was acting as a barrier to anyone that might try to enter. He was protecting her, acting as a guard to keep her safe.

A short time later, Orna and the other women returned, each carrying large buckets of steaming water. Orna set hers down and came to stand by Maggie. Holding up a clean dress, she measured it against Maggie's frame. "Aye, I think this will fit fine."

Just then the laird entered the room carrying the basin tub.

Maggie's breath hitched. He looked at her with warm eyes and a bright smile as he placed it on the floor near the fire.

His smiled warmed her as much as the sun shining down on her skin. But the warmth he radiated started from her belly. He made her feel like a jewel to be treasured.

"I hope ye enjoy yer bath, my lady. Mayhap later, after ye bathe and sup, we can speak further."

"I would like that."

He gave her a slight bow before turning on his heel and walking out the door.

Maggie's heart beat like a drum in her chest as he passed near her. A steady thrum that could be made into song. In no way was he threatening, her reaction was visceral. Even in her state, wounded as she was, her body jumped to life. As if awakening after a long nap. A sense of peace settled into her weary bones, and she relished feeling.

Orna's close presence, her hand rubbing calming circles on her skin, was an added comfort and reassured Maggie she had nothing to fear from the people here.

The laird was even bigger than Diel. With him so close, his massive size could have been off-putting, but it had the opposite effect. His sheer size and caring mannerisms solidified her safety, as if he were a stone wall to protect her from the ravages of a trebuchet.

Whereas Diel was dark and brooding and ominous, this man was light and open and accommodating.

After the tub was filled, the maids left, closing the door behind them, leaving Maggie alone with Orna once again.

"Come, my lady, let's get ye out of this dirty shift." She took the throw and placed it at the foot of the bed. "Take me hands for balance and stand up."

"I would rather undress myself," Maggie said quietly, her gaze fixed on her dirty feet. No one had ever helped her bathe a day in her life, and she didn't feel like starting now. Already over the past sennight all the control over her own body had been taken. At least with this, the cleaning of her own body, she wasn't to feel autonomous.

Orna gave her a strong smile that reflected respect and nodded her head. "I'll tell ye what, let's get ye settled in the tub and seated safely, and then ye can take yer shift off. It doesna matter if it gets wet, we are going to launder it anyhow."

Maggie smiled, relieved that Orna didn't push her, and stood gingerly. The pain in her feet radiated up her legs. Keeping one hand on Maggie's arm to keep her steady, they maneuvered their way to the basin and Orna helped Maggie slowly ease into the steaming water. She relished the luxury at the same time trying to ignore the stinging burn of her many cuts.

"I'll turn around, my lady, and give ye yer privacy."

Maggie reached down into the water and grabbed the hem of the shift, slowly and gently pulling it up and over her head, she placed the item over the side of the tub. She sat cradling her knees, thankful the water was high enough that it covered her breasts making her more comfortable at not being fully exposed. She told Orna she could turn around.

The woman's sharp intake of breath at the sight of

Maggie's bruises that were a stark contrast of color against her pale skin. "My lady," Orna whispered. "I'm so sorry."

Maggie bent her head, mortified of her appearance, and remained silent. She didn't trust herself to not break out in tears. All she'd been able to see was what was done to the front of her body, but if her back looked just as bad...

"Whoever did this to ye should be flayed alive and salt rubbed into the wounds. 'Tis not right. Was it yer husband?" Orna asked.

Maggie shook her head. "Nay, I've never been wed."

"Ye poor thing. I ken naught what has happened to ye. Ye are strong to have survived. The beast will meet his fate, I'm sure." She tsked as she reached into a box and came away with a handful of dried purple flowers, dropping the petals into the water. "Lavender. 'Twill soothe yer skin and leave a beautiful scent."

Maggie breathed in deep the glorious fragrance. She'd never been provided such a luxury before.

"Put yer head back, my lady. I'll wash yer hair."

Orna's offering was akin to the treatment of a queen. The offer made Maggie feel special. Deserving, which was so foreign to her after the way she'd spent the last sennight. But it wasn't something she wanted right now. "I dinna mean to offend. I appreciate yer offer. But if ye dinna mind, I'd prefer to do so myself." She held her breath, waiting for Orna's response, afraid of seeming ungrateful. "Mayhap at a later time," she added.

"Och, lass. How insensitive of me. Of course, ye dinna want someone, a stranger of all people, touching ye in such a way." She reached over to the table and grabbed a cup. "Here, for yer hair."

"Thank ye." Maggie accepted the proffered cup, along with a small square of cloth and a bar of hard soap scented with herbs. She brought the bar to her nose and inhaled deeply. The fragrance pleasantly tickling her nose. She and her parents usually kept the herbs they collected to sell. Scented bar soap was a luxury they couldn't afford.

While Maggie slowly washed the dirt and blood from her hair and body as best she could, Orna kept her back to her, prattling along as she busied herself around the room.

Maggie tenderly worked her fingers through the snarls in her hair that hadn't been brushed since Diel had captured her. She worried that they would be too big, and she would have to shear her hair off to rid herself of the knots. But she took her time and finally managed to work them out and was able to wash her hair thoroughly.

"Dinna let the size of our new laird fool ye," the woman continued as she moved about. "I've known him since he was a lad. He's been away for a verra long time, but when he arrived with ye in his arms, I could see he's still a gentle soul."

He definitely has Orna's favor.

Maggie listened as Orna continued talking. She took solace in the woman's rambling as she carefully used the square of cloth to clean the many cuts over her body, all in various stages of healing.

"'Tis not been easy for him. The clan doesna know what to think of him. He was never meant to be our leader," Orna continued. "I think he'll do a find job, but others may question him. He'll prove them wrong, dinna ye fash about that."

The way Orna talked about the new laird, Maggie could tell she was truly enamored with the man. She wondered why some of the clan didn't feel the same way.

She understood he wasn't supposed to be laird, but he seemed very capable of leading to her. She'd only seen him with a few people, but he seemed to have no issue taking charge. And he was constantly assessing his surroundings, whether it came to her or the room they were in. He was always observing.

A good leader needed to be observant.

Or maybe she was seeing more to him than was there because he saved her from possible death and brought her here to heal.

Maggie only hoped he'd understand when she left once she was fully healed. Because she couldn't stay. As much as she might one day enjoy the pampering, she would have her revenge against Diel first. When she was strong enough, she would leave to find that bloody bastard. She didn't care how long it took her to learn who and where he was. She would find out.

It was a vow to herself she would see through to fruition.

And when she did, she'd make sure he breathed no more.

CHAPTER 6

*B*roderick was impressed with how well the lass was handling her current situation. He knew, just by the evidence of what she'd experienced, that it was horrific, and she'd somehow found herself in much worse situations.

He didn't know what exactly had happened. *Yet.* He would find out. It struck him that he still didn't know her name. Something he would have to rectify in their next meeting.

"Broderick?" Alastair broke into his thoughts as he quickened his pace to catch up to him. "Ye alright?"

"Aye, my mind is muddled in thoughts today." He knew something that would occupy his mind for some time and free him from the hold of the lass. "Ye up for a ride?"

Alastair gaze swept out over the sea and shrugged. "Sure. Where are we headed?"

"I want to see the area where Ewan and father were ambushed." He knew it had been some time since the killings and any trace of who had done the deed would be gone, but he still wanted to see it for himself.

"Of course."

They made their way to the stables and Goliath huffed his happiness at seeing Broderick.

"There's my strong beastie," Broderick said affectionately as he ran a hand down the horse's black mane. "Have they been taking good care of ye?" Goliath nuzzled his hand before bobbing his head. The two had a special connection. There were times when Goliath had felt like his only friend.

"I have my laird!" The same boy who had cared for Goliath the night before popped up from another stall.

"What 'tis yer name, lad?"

"Dearg, my laird."

"Weel, thank ye verra much, Dearg." Broderick ruffled the boy's hair before turning his attention back to Goliath.

They got the horses ready and made their way to the spot of the incident. Today, the weather was temperate, but the recent rains made the ground muddy and the needles from the pine trees on the forest floor made a rustic, fragrant mix that filled Broderick's senses. His muscles were stiff. The tension of the past few days was catching up to him. It was all too much.

His father and brother's deaths. Becoming laird. Finding the lass. His life had taken a drastic turn and he was still unsure how he felt about it.

And there was a killer and a ravager of women out there walking the earth. Breathing the very air he did. Broderick needed to find both men and make them pay for what they've done.

The two men rode in silence until they reached the area where Callum and Ewan had been struck down.

They hadn't ridden far when Alastair whistled and slowed his horse and Broderick did the same.

"Here?" Broderick asked, his brow furrowed.

Alastair nodded, his mouth in a grim line.

""Tis much closer than I expected."

Broderick was surprised at the location. It was closer to Straik then he expected.

He was unsure why, but he just figured the hunting party had been deep into MacLeod lands when the ambush happened. But they were upon the scene of the attack before long. He could almost see Straik from this distance. Not quite, but he felt he could if he really tried. That's how close they were. Granted, the castle was surrounded on three sides by forest, but he questioned why they wouldn't hunt a little further out. He sat upon Goliath for a few long moments, surveying the area.

The trees were hearty, and a thick blanket of pine needles and orange and brown leaves covered the ground. The scent of pine hung heavy in the air.

"Who planned the hunt?"

"Ewan set this hunt up."

Well, that shot down Broderick's thought of an ambush from someone inside the castle. Ewan wouldn't have planned his own murder.

"Yer father and brother were facing south at the time of the attack," Alastair offered. "The arrows flew from that direction straight at them through the trees."

Broderick nodded and dismounted, giving Goliath a pat before he walked around the area, taking in the surroundings.

It had been too long since the attack and as he expected, there was nothing of use to be found.

"Damn bastards," Broderick cursed. Not only were they scourge for attacking a party out on a hunt, but they were also cowards for shooting them in hiding. They didn't have the bollocks to show their faces to the men as they killed them. The two men deserved the opportunity to fight for their lives.

He studied the ground where his father and brother were standing when the arrows were shot through the trees.

"Shite," he spat, toeing the dead leaves with this boot, disturbing the earth to see if could find something, anything, knowing it was no use. He faced south and traced what he thought would be the trajectory of the arrows when they were launched.

What was the reason for the slayings? Had his father gotten into bad dealings? Owed debt? Nay, that didn't track.

Broderick walked deeper into the woods, his eyes studying the ground with each step.

It seemed unlikely the clan owed money to anyone. His father was an arse, and from what he'd heard about Ewan, his brother was following in their father's footsteps well, but Callum always paid his debts. If anything, people owed him money. Mayhap someone didn't want to pay. Murdering the laird would be a daft move in that case. The money was owed to the clan, not the laird. His death didn't cancel the debt.

Broderick didn't see any of his clansmen executing such a plan. Why would they? He treated his people well.

Something didn't sit right with Broderick, but he couldn't put his finger on it. He was missing something. He could feel it course through his veins. Why would someone want his father and brother dead? It seemed a power grab. If it was a land grab the attackers would have killed the whole hunting party and then stormed Straik. But that didn't happen.

Even though Broderick held no real affection for his father and brother, neither of the men deserved to be cut down the way they were. Without a chance to stave off their attackers. Their lack of a relationship didn't lessen his duty. No matter what, the MacLeod was murdered, and that act needed to be responded to.

Broderick would avenge his father and brother. His clan expected nothing less from him.

There had been no claims to the holdings or the lands since the deaths, so mayhap it wasn't a power grab. But that's the only thing that made sense.

Standing in a small cluster of trees that would have offered ample cover, Broderick turned and looked to where his brother and father would have been standing at the time of the attack. He lifted his arm as if he were holding a bow and notched and invisible arrow and pulled back. He had plenty of room to both stay hidden and let the arrow fly. Eyeing the ground, as suspected, he found no sign of whoever the killer was or anyone else being in the particular spot.

However, this area was too small for two men. So, either the killer was a lightning quick shot or there was more than one archer that day at a different place in the woods.

Broderick would say the latter if he had to guess. Less room for error. He scanned the woods and found another copse of trees a few paces away that would offer the same coverage while still giving the archer an advantageous spot.

"I think mayhap there were two attackers," Broderick stated.

"'Twould make sense. I had thought the same."

He strode over to the other possible hiding space. Like the other, it was just big enough to notch an arrow and let it fly, but it offered the same amount of coverage.

Once again, he found nothing. Nothing but leaves and broken twigs that could have been from men or any one of the wild animals that ran through these woods.

"They would have had to lay in wait for the hunting party. They could have sat here for hours. Who could have wanted the MacLeod dead that badly?"

The archers could shoot their arrows, see their targets fall, and then escape deeper into the woods while the clansmen were busy trying to figure out what happened. The scenario was perfect.

Alastair shrugged. "I've asked myself that verra question over and over. I dinna ken."

Another question nagged at Broderick. "How did they know?" The hunting grounds weren't a secret, but someone not in their clan wouldn't have the inside knowledge of where exactly they would be. "Do ye think there is a traitor in the clan?"

Alastair sighed. "There have been rumors. Someone out there wanted them dead for certain."

"What have ye heard?"

Broderick's mentor shrugged. "One of yer father's former guards, Liam, was relieved of his duties a few weeks ago, right before the ambush."

That caught Broderick's attention. "Why for? And why am I just hearing about this now?"

"'Tis just a rumor. He was caught lifting coin from yer father's coffers. He could have lost his hand. But yer father, as mad as he was, didna do that. He removed him from his post and said he couldna work for him any longer. Liam was upset, but thankful, knowing what the consequences could have been. I heard he's found work with the blacksmith."

"Interesting."

"Aye, but not a strong enough lead to warrant wasting our efforts when we need to find the real killer."

Broderick nodded. "Mayhap someone is feeding information to an unknown enemy for reasons yet to be revealed." Broderick commented. Again, it was something Broderick could not fathom, not with how well-liked Callum was within the clan.

A pheasant swooped down and landed in the middle of the clearing, pecking its beak into the earth in search of a meal.

With the visit failing to provide any answers, Broderick gave a final glance at the area and then walked over to where Goliath waited patiently. The pheasant let out a squawk of irritation before flying away.

"Let us return to the keep. I told the lass I would visit again later. I'm itching to get back to her."

"Ye've taken a fondness to her?" Alastair inquired curiously.

Broderick shrugged. "I find her a mystery I want to solve."

"Do ye not think 'tis quite the coincidence that yer father and brother are killed and then this lass is found shortly thereafter?" Alastair asked Broderick as they rode along the southwestern perimeter curtain wall on their way back to Straik Castle.

"What are ye implying?"

Alastair shrugged. "I dinna ken. It seems odd to me. Straik isna a hotspot for reivers and it hasna been raided in years. The MacLeod are too strong and mighty. Yet within a span of days, we have an ambush that leads to two deaths and the almost death of a strange woman found near MacLeod woods."

"Do ye think whoever killed my father and brother is the same person that attacked the lady?" Broderick refused to believe that Alastair was heading in the direction of thinking the lass was involved somehow.

"Mayhap. 'Twould seem so if ye think about it. Or mayhap, whoever did it knew she wouldna perish and could provide them with clan information."

"Nay. That makes no sense, Alastair. She doesna appear to have any interest in my affairs. She's too consumed with trying to heal. As she should be."

Alastair stopped and narrowed his eyes as he studied Broderick. "Ye trust the lass already?"

"I dinna think she was abandoned in the woods for nefarious reasons against the clan. She was brutalized. I ken whoever hurt her hoped she would perish in the woods and no one would ever know."

Alastair continued walking. "Men that do such crimes need to be dealt with."

"Aye, and he will be as soon as I find out who it is."

"I've no doubt in that, my laird."

Broderick grunted at the moniker and shook his head. "She has a package that she is guarding."

"A package?"

"Aye. 'Tis wee. I've naught idea what it may be. The lass had hidden it in her bedding, but it dropped to the floor when the maids were changing the linens. When it happened, she paled even more than she already was, which I didna think was possible. A family heirloom she managed to keep a hold of, mayhap." He could understand that. Wanting to hold on to something that reminded one of a loved one no longer walking the earth.

Broderick did wonder if the two instances were related. The thought was plausible. He just didn't know the why's of it all. She had piqued his interest, though he wanted to know what she was hiding.

They paused by a battered spot in the curtain wall where stones had fallen and left an opening in the barrier and peered at the damage. It looked like it had been caused by age and weather. Nothing in the surrounding thick forest gave any clue to another conclusion.

"That will need to be fixed sooner rather than later," Broderick stated. "With unknown attackers out there, we dinna need to offer easy entry into Straik's walls. We havena been raided yet. I dinna want it to happen now that I'm here."

Alastair nodded. "Ye can send some men out here when we get back."

Broderick raised a brow in question. "I could if I knew

enough about my men to ken which ones were handy with masonry and building."

"I can help ye with that. They're working on the new tower. Just send a couple of them out here and all will be good."

They continued on along the perimeter of MacLeod lands. The thick blanket of pine, willow, and birch trees thinned to a singular row of sycamore trees that led to the entrance gate.

"Ye make it sound so easy, Alastair."

"Och, afore long ye'll be running Straik as if ye were always meant to be its laird.

Broderick scoffed at the idea. "Next ye will be telling me I need a wife."

Alastair's look confirmed Broderick's thought.

"Nay. Absolutely no'. I've enough with having to lead the clan, run Straik, and avenge my family to worry about a wife and bairns." And avenge the unknown lass currently healing at Straik. He wouldn't mind finding a lass with her strength for a wife. She'd been through so much and yet she prevailed. Never gave up. She was headstrong and full of grit and determination.

Alastair opened his mouth to say something, and Broderick cut him off before he had the chance.

"Dinna tell me that ye werena going to say that, because that is the natural progression. Wife, then bairns." He kicked Goliath into a trot. "I will tell ye this, when I am blessed with bairns, I'll be damned sure not to subject them to the childhood I had. Laird or no', my sons will be shown love and worth from both parents."

Nodding, Alastair smiled in agreement, but said nothing as he kept pace with Broderick as they turned their horses toward the castle.

They finished the journey in silence. Broderick heard the water running ashore, smelled the salt in the air.

The leaves on the trees lining the outside wall were changing colors. Vibrant oranges, reds, and yellows. Soon, they would fall to the ground and create a colorful blanket that swathed the grounds. Late-season flowers were in bloom in the garden. Perennials his mother had planted years ago.

She'd loved these grounds.

Did the lass like flowers? It would be nice to have someone enjoy them once again.

It would bring renewed life to Straik. He had a feeling since his mother had been gone, the women of the clan hadn't had an easy life. He wasn't certain that was the case. But from what he'd witnessed so far, the women he'd seen seemed weary, defeated almost.

He would change that.

He'd left Straik a few years after his mother had passed, and in that time, he remembered his father coercing some of the women into his bed. Mostly serving wenches. He had no idea if the behavior continued after her left, but he knew is father never remarried.

After a long stretch of silence, Alastair asked, "Are ye feeling better with yer current circumstances?"

Broderick let out a bark of laughter. "That's what we're calling this. A good number of lasses are frightened of me. Some of the men dinna trust me. Though Dearg seems to be quite enamored with me," he answered with a smile.

"Give them time. Dearg's a good lad. Wants nothing more than to help out where he can. Which is more than I can say for his useless father."

"Ye ken who his father is?"

"I do, but he doesna. Because his mother wants to keep it

that way, but 'tis no secret around the castle. The bastard is never here anyway. He's too busy running games from town to town. I'm sure that Dearg's mother wasna the first to be seduced by his wily charm and I'm sure she willna be the last."

He knew it was common, but it never sat right with Broderick. If he knew he'd fathered a child, he'd take responsibility for that child. A man wasn't forced to marry the lass if he didn't want to, but if he had any character, he should at the very least, claim the child.

But that was not the protocol. The child was destined to be a bastard.

From what little Broderick had seen of Dearg thus far, he seemed to be too good of a lad to be burdened with such a label. He made a mental note to take the boy under his tutelage. Broderick may have not been taught all of what was needed to be laird, and didn't have experience leading large numbers of men, but he'd done enough leading of small groups in his life to be able to make it work.

"On the morrow, I'll start with training the men. I need to see where they are at in their skills. Hopefully that will build some trust and camaraderie."

Alastair dipped his head. "I think it may. 'Tis a start anyway. I know ye have the qualities needed. Ye just need to prove it to them."

"Aye," Broderick answered, but deep down, he wondered if he could successfully lead the clan.

Right now, his priorities were being dragged in separate directions—leading the clan and protecting the lass. He was thankful Orna was there for her, but he wanted to be the one there. The one she leaned on. The one she turned to when she needed help.

Hell, he barely knew the lass and his mind was wandering into dangerous territory. He didn't even know her name for Christ's sake.

He had the sudden urge to meet with the lass. Surely, she had finished with her bath and filled her stomach.

In the stables, Broderick hopped off Goliath and grabbed an apple out of a crate in the corner and fed it the horse, then handed the reins over to the stable hand.

"We can talk later about the repairs." He clapped Alastair on the back and began walking in the direction of the keep.

"Where are ye off to?"

Broderick turned to face Alastair but didn't stop. Instead, he walked backwards. "To go see the lass." He gave his mentor a wide smile before spinning on his heel and all but jogged to the courtyard.

A few clansmen acknowledged him with a dip of their heads as he passed.

Mayhap Alastair was right. His clan was accepting him.

ALONE IN HER ROOM, Maggie reached into the small hole in the mattress that she'd made by widening an already present cut. She pulled out the brooch that she'd found in the woods. The silver needed a good shining to bring the luster back to it, but the eagle design was still clearly visible. The brooch symbolized everything she loathed.

And right now, it was the only piece of information that she had that would help her identify where to locate Diel and his men.

With more rest, she'll regain her strength more and more every day, and she hoped that soon she'll be well enough to leave this place and hunt the bastard down. Maggie would make Diel pay for the hell he'd put her through. The attack on her village. The deaths of her friends and fellow villagers. The death of life as she knew it.

Maggie would avenge every single one of them.

She'd raze his keep to the ground and as he watched it burn, she'd strike him down. The thought of seeing the brute being brought to his knees by the very person he'd savagely treated for his sadistic entertainment made her smile, a sliver of satisfaction sidling up her spine.

But she had to get strong first. She had to heal. She hadn't seen her reflection since before she'd been taken, but she didn't need one to know how bruised and swollen her face was. She felt it every time she spoke or gave the faintest smile. Could tell it with her limited vision due to her right eye still being so swollen from Diel's punches.

Each hour that passed, she grew stronger. Healed a little more. Each day away from Diel was a day that her body thrived. Readying itself for her day of reckoning.

She would need to learn how to fight. Diel was strong. She'd be naïve if she thought she could just arrive at his castle and end his life.

The clang of metal against metal sounded outside the window. The screech of steel bringing her back to that day.

She remembered the attack as clearly as if it were happening all over again. She was running to the woods after Diel and his men attacked, striking down anyone they came across and setting fire to the thatched roof cottages of her village.

The smoke was thick in the air, filling Maggie's lungs as she ran. The screams of her fellow villagers loud in her ears. The edge of the forest was just ahead. She was almost there, when she was grabbed roughly from behind.

Without seeing who it was, she rounded her arm, her small dirk fisted in her hand. The blade met its target. She felt the sickening dip as it sank into flesh, and she dragged her hand down.

The brute let out a howl before grabbing her wrist and squeezing until she cried out in pain, dropping the knife into the peat. She got a glimpse of his dark features, black eyes, angry as a demon, a wound oozing blood from his cheekbone to his jaw, moments before he drew his hand back and brought it down to slap it across her cheek.

The sheer force of the hit reeled her back and she fell onto her bottom, eyes wide with fear.

He scooped her up and threw her over his shoulder and onto his horse. She didn't know how long they rode, the whole time he cursed at her, telling her she would pay for what she'd done.

And she did.

A soft knock sounded, startling Maggie back to the present. Maggie opened her eyes again, the memory fading. She took a deep breath as she looked around the room, reminding herself that she was safe. She was in the MacLeod castle, away from Diel for now.

And revenge would be hers. There was no other way this was going to end. Even if she died in the process, knowing she took Diel with her was all she needed.

Once she was stronger, then she could plan her attack.

She swiped at the tears that had slipped out of her eyes and down her cheeks as Orna poked her head in the room.

"My lady, may I come in?" she asked quietly.

Maggie sniffed and nodded, quickly shoving the brooch in the pocket of her dress and watched as the woman entered and tried to shut the door behind her.

She couldn't though. In the doorway, stood the laird. "How are ye faring, lass?" His brows furrowed when he looked at her.

Could he tell she was upset?

"My laird. Shoo." The woman waved her hands, but he didn't budge.

"'Tis alright, Orna." The words were out of Maggie's mouth before she knew what she was saying.

Two pairs of surprised eyes stared at her.

"My lady?"

"Laird MacLeod can come in. He'd stated earlier he would be by later. I feel better now. We can speak if ye'd like."

And she did, even if she'd briefly lost herself in memories. Waves of concern radiated off the laird. They washed over her like an angry ocean. His reaction was comforting. This warrior. This man that she'd met only days ago showed more care for her well-being than Diel had ever shown her. That monster didn't have a caring bone in his body.

But Laird MacLeod? He had a genuine soul. His large stature didn't frighten her. It made her feel protected, and she was so thankful for that.

She knew her appearance was better than earlier now that she'd had a bath. Her hair was washed, and one of the maids had brushed her thick locks until they shone before loosely plaiting it and coiling it into a bun. She was careful to not pull too tight and make it uncomfortable. Maggie was still in awe at the kindness she'd been shown.

But her nerves still jumped, and she willed her breath to calm.

Orna gave a stern look to the laird but waved him into the room. "If it's alright with ye, my laird, I'll stay and work tidying the room whilst ye two talk."

Laird MacLeod nodded and focused his attention on Maggie, his blue gaze locking with hers.

Maggie knew Orna couldn't give orders to the laird, but she was thankful for her meddling ways to offer her support. The laird wasn't threatening when he entered the room. He softened his demeanor by rounding his shoulders and the gesture somehow made him seem less imposing. "Thank ye, Orna."

The laird didn't look upset that Orna was staying, and once again, Maggie was presented with the difference between this man and Diel.

Maggie smiled, the gesture sending jolts of pain through her face, but she ignored them.

"My laird," she said once Orna busied herself with the items on the table in the far corner.

"Ye can call me Broderick."

A strong name for a strong man. She'd already heard Orna say the laird's name, but the way it fell from his lips made it seem even stronger.

"Maggie," she heard herself say. She just realized that she'd never told Orna her name and she saw the woman beam at her at the declaration. The woman had only called her my lady, so she supposed there wasn't a need. But she didn't want the laird to call her that. She wasn't a lady. Far from it.

"Maggie," he repeated, his deep timbre rolling over her. "And yer surname?"

Of course, he would want to know that. As she didn't fully trust him, neither did he trust her yet. He'd want to know if she was from an ally or warring clan. But she knew he was a MacLeod.

Yet, she still wasn't ready to disclose that information to him. "My lai--Broderick. I mean nay disrespect, but at this time, I wouldna like to say," she answered.

He narrowed his blue eyes, studying her for a moment.

What was he thinking?

"Weel, Maggie of unknown surname, 'tis an honor to make yer acquaintance."

IF BRODERICK DIDN'T KNOW any better, he would not have thought the lass sitting in front of him was the same lass from the woods.

Her bruised face made him want to punch something, preferably the heathen that had attacked her.

But he could see her eyes, well, eye. Her right eye was still quite swollen, but he could make out the sky-blue of the eye looking up at him. Her hair wasn't chestnut colored as he'd originally thought. Nay, instead it was the color of the finest honey. And it was coiled neatly at her slender nape. The bruises at her neck were an angry yellow.

She was dressed in a soft woolen dress that fit loosely so as not to aggravate her wounds.

"Were ye able to sup?" He had so many questions but didn't think bombarding her with them all at once was the right approach.

"Aye, thank ye. Orna and everyone I've met have been most kind."

Broderick smiled, glad he and the clan were able to offer some relief.

"Ye're sitting near the window again." It was a statement, but also a question. The air was slightly cool, especially now that the sun was setting, and he was sure she would get chilled afore long.

She looked up, wincing at the movement, and pain pierced his gut at her suffering. "I like feeling the sun upon my skin and the smell of fresh air."

Had she been kept away from light and fresh air? In a dungeon? Is she an escaped prisoner? He doubted that very much. "Winter will be here, and 'twill be too cold to do so soon."

She nodded, acknowledging that truth. "Where am I?"

He hid his smile. So, the lass was just as curious as he was. "Straik Castle."

She looked confused. "I'm afraid I dinna ken where that is. I never left my village before..." her voice trailed off.

He wanted to ask before what but knew he couldn't force

that from her. She needed to be ready to tell him. Instead, he decided to tell her about Straik. "Straik has been in my family for years. Near the bay." He looked toward the window. "'Tis a shame ye're not in one of the rooms located on the other side of the castle. Ye can hear the ocean from there. Smell the salt of the sea."

Maggie blessed him with a small smile, that he was sure pained her. "Sounds lovely."

"It is. Mayhap we'll see about having yer room moved to another once ye feel up to the task."

"Oh, ye dinna have to do that. I dinna want to impose and ye've done so much already." She wrung her hands together, fretting.

He ground his teeth. He knew she was strong, but he also knew she was broken. The knowledge of that sliced through him and it took all his composure to keep his hands still and not fist them and strike the wall.

"'Tis no trouble, lass. The clan has seen much tragedy these past few weeks. I think they are happy fer the distraction."

Her brows furrowed. "Tragedy?"

"Aye," he toyed with how much he should tell her, but in the end, her reaction would tell him everything he needed to know. "My father and brother were attacked recently."

Her eyes rounded. "How do they fare?"

The question was genuine. Her face showed no sign of deception.

"No' well. Both were killed."

Her sharp intake of breath started a fit of coughs and he caught himself before he rushed to her side. But Orna was there in a flash.

"Och, my lady. Easy. Small breaths."

Maggie looked at him with watery eyes once her breathing had eased back to normal and she sat back gingerly in the chair. "I'm sorry for yer loss." She dabbed at the corners of her eyes with the linen Orna handed to her. "What happened?" She asked and then looked to the floor shamefully. "If ye dinna mind me asking. I dinna mean to pry."

"They were attacked in the woods. On a hunt."

Her blonde head snapped up and her eyes fixed on his. Eyes round in fear. The lass was deathly afraid. That wasn't his intention.

"Dinna fear, Maggie. Ye are safe here."

She began to shiver, and Orna tsked as she retrieved another throw and tucked it around Maggie's shoulders.

The woman was terrified, and he didn't think it was of him. She was genuinely surprised to learn his father and brother had been attacked and killed. Could both attacks have been perpetrated by the same person?

Broderick couldn't control fisting his hands at the thought. He took in a deep breath and relaxed his hands before he frightened the lass even further. He stood and gave her a slight bow. "I'll leave ye to Orna's care. Thank ye for talking with me. I do hope ye truly feel safe here, lass. I will no' let any harm come to ye."

Before opening the door, he turned and asked, "Can I visit ye again in the morn?" He hoped she would say yes, but would grant her wish if it was no.

"Aye," she said, her voice barely above a whisper.

He nodded and gave her a warm smile. "Rest well, lass. The morrow brings a new day."

When he pulled the door open, he looked over his shoulder before he left the room. Orna had Maggie enveloped in warm embrace. As he thought, she was right there providing the support that Maggie needed. He was glad that the healer had taken such a liking to the lass.

He was certain she needed someone on her side.

Broderick was on her side, though he didn't think she realized that or was ready to admit it yet.

She would. Eventually. He would prove to her that he'd help her in any way that he could.

He looked forward to the day she learned she could trust him.

CHAPTER 7

*M*aggie watched the laird leave and was thankful that he hadn't pressed her for more information. She would tell him all that had happened, but she wasn't ready to reveal that information yet. Nor was she ready for the pain speaking about it would bring.

Her heart longed for her parents. Ached for her village. For all the innocent lives lost in the attack.

It seemed she and Broderick were both in mourning.

Orna wrapped her in a warm hug, her bony arms surprisingly strong, a concerned look on her face.

"Are ye all right, my lady?"

"I am, thank ye." Maggie knew Orna had no idea how much her hug meant to her right now. There were days where she longed for the hugs she used to receive from her parents.

"Laird MacLeod didna upset ye overmuch, did he? I'll make sure he doesna do it again."

"Nay. Just my own memories."

"Memories of the past can be painful, indeed. We can only

take solace in the fact that our loved ones are in a happier place."

Maggie nodded but remained silent. Truer words couldn't be spoken. Maggie's saving grace was knowing her parents were together on the other side. Even though she missed them so, she was happy for that.

Maggie could only hope to find a love as strong as theirs one day.

"Och, then, why dinna we get ye ready for bed? Do ye think ye can walk or should I call for help?"

"I can walk." She wasn't sure if she could, but she didn't want Orna bringing in the laird to help move her when he'd just left. She felt an inexplicable pull to the man when he was near. He was understanding, compassionate. She found him to be well-mannered and gentle, always taking her feelings into consideration. She knew Orna was enamored with Broderick. And mayhap if circumstances were different, Maggie would be able to do the same. Mayhap she just needed more time.

Nay.

She feared that the more time she spent with the laird, the easier he would be to talk to. She had to remain vigilant. She needed to stay strong and keep her mind on what mattered the most—finding Diel. But Broderick was kind. She didn't believe that he wasn't showing his true self to her. Or was she looking too much into his actions because he's the one that saved her in the woods? Mayhap her view of him was skewed because of that.

She also didn't want the laird to think she was depending on him for everything. She needed to learn how to stand on her own. Figuratively and physically. For how else would she get to Diel?

She slowly stood, using Orna's bony shoulder as support,

and gingerly took a step. Pain shot up her legs and she sucked in her breath.

"Easy, my lady. No need to rush."

Maggie took her time. Taking small steps until she finally reached the bed. Orna helped her ease onto the padding and get settled. She retrieved the pitcher and poured a glass of water and set it on the small table near the bed.

"I'll bring ye in a nice, hot cup of tea. I'll add something that will help ye sleep, too," Orna winked as she left the room.

Maggie looked forward to a night of sleep where she didn't have to worry about being attacked or set upon by Diel. She'd been away from him for a few nights, but it was hard to leave that worry in the past.

A good night's sleep and a meeting with the laird again in the morning?

That was something to look forward to.

AFTER ANOTHER LONG night spent in the same room he'd had as a child, morn and the time to break his fast couldn't come soon enough. The chamber only brought back memories Broderick didn't want to think about. The wooden bench in the corner his father used to beat him over. The bed with its dark mahogany wood was marred from all the times Callum had hit the posts with whatever he decided to whip Broderick with.

Once he got settled, he'd have new furniture built and move into the master chamber. He needed to go through his father's belongings and eventually his brother's, but it was not a task he looked forward to doing. He couldn't delay for too long. He needed to get an understanding of the books and where the clan stood financially.

He washed his face in the basin, the water ice cold after sitting out all night, then ran the water through his hair and slicked it back from his face. It didn't matter, as soon as it dried, it would be in his face again as always.

Once dressed, he made his way down into the kitchens, taking the back steps, and entered the same way he used to sneak in when he was a young lad. The kitchen wenches were busy preparing the food for the day's meals, and most ignored him as he walked through.

The few that spared a glance toward him, he gave a smile, and they returned the gesture before resuming their preparations. He was feeling better about his newfound position and the people it included.

He still had work to do with those that looked at him with questions in their eyes. He understood that.

Trust was earned. He just had to learn what would put them at ease and put their trust in him. He had to show them that he could lead their clan. Right now, they had nothing to base their opinion on except for the boy he'd been when he left, and the stories told to them by Callum.

He'd grown into a successful man since then. He'd prove his worth to the clan.

In the Great Hall, Alastair sat at a table, a mug of ale and a crust of bread in a trencher set in front of him. He and Orna were deep in conversation. She saw him approach and gave him a slightly unsteady bow, using the tabletop for balance.

"My laird. Good morn. I hope ye are settling back into yer home after a few days here."

He dipped his head in greeting and smiled. "Orna, good morn to ye. It's been a verra long time since I've called Straik Castle home. But I'm settling fine, thank ye."

"Good. The clan, now more than ever, needs a leader. There's no one better than ye to guide them." She patted him on the arm. "We need ye need to be the strength of the

MacLeod. We need ye to show that the actions taken against us will no' be tolerated."

"All in due time, Orna. My family will be avenged. I've given my vow that they will be."

He looked at Alastair. "I've some ideas for what can be done. We can discuss strategy later."

Alastair nodded in agreement and washed down his last bite of bread with a swig of ale.

Switching from clan business to something more personal—the lass. "How is Maggie this morn? Was her night better than the last?" He asked nonchalantly. He didn't want them to know that she'd occupied much of his thoughts the previous night.

"Aye. The lady is still in pain, but she is faring better than I expected. She's strong, that one. Has the streak of a fighter in her."

He agreed. It was a miracle she survived in the woods. How long had she been out there? Broderick clenched his fists, tightening his mouth into a grim line. From the information she'd provided him with the previous night, he believed she'd been taken from her village during an attack. She hadn't quite said as much. But the way she'd stopped abruptly and got that frightened, faraway look in her eyes, it was easy to guess.

"Have there been any recent village attacks that ye are aware of?"

"Nay, none that I've heard."

Broderick rubbed his chin, deep in thought. He didn't know how long Maggie been held, but he could imagine the horrors she'd suffered. Memories of his sweet mother flooded his mind. The pain she'd suffered at the hands of his father. To think the lass endured the same treatment, mayhap worse, made Broderick's blood boil.

"Has she broken her fast? I'll bring her something to eat."

"She's already eaten, my laird."

He dipped his head in acknowledgement. "'Tis fine. I promised her a visit this morn." He snatched a chunk of bread off the table and popped a bite into his mouth.

"My laird. Dinna stay long. She needs her rest."

He flashed Orna a wide smile and gave her a wink. "Understood. 'Twill be a quick visit."

OUTSIDE MAGGIE'S DOOR, Broderick knocked and waited.

"Aye?"

Her voice was barely audible through the thick wood of the door.

He pushed it open and poked his head in. "Good morn, my lady. May I come in? I'll leave the door open." He doubted she would want to be alone in a closed room with him just yet.

Maggie nodded. "Thank ye."

He dipped his head in acknowledgement and entered the room. She was sitting in the chair near the window again. She looked better today. Her blonde hair braided and coiled at her nape. The swelling in her face had gone down and he could see both of her eyes. Big, round eyes blue as the sea. Her high cheekbones were still bruised, but they were more prominent now that the swelling had gone down.

"Ye look well."

She let out a small laugh. "Ye dinna need to flatter me, my laird. I know 'tis not true."

"Please call me Broderick. There's no need for formalities. I speak the truth. Yer color is better today. Ye dinna look so pale."

She flinched when he said that, and he furrowed his brows. "Did I say something wrong, lass?"

Maggie shook her head. "Nay. Ye just," she paused, rolling her bottom lip under her teeth, "that just reminded me of a conversation from the past."

He wished she would open up to him. He wanted to press her, to force her to tell him. But he knew that this was something she couldn't be pushed on. Whatever ordeal she had been through, she needed to tell it on her own terms. Until she was ready, he would be here showing her the comfort and understanding he believed she needed.

"I apologize. I dinna mean to bring up painful memories. How are ye feeling this morn?" He best change the topic. He didn't want to see her cry nor be the cause.

She looked grateful for the new direction. "Everything still hurts, but less than before."

"That's good. No' that everything still hurts, but that ye feel yer pain is lessened. Orna can work wonders with her healing powers. I'm glad she's still here."

"Was she going to leave?"

"Nay, I dinna think so. I've just arrived back at Straik after being away for many years. She was the healer here when I was a lad. She seemed ancient to me back then. I had thought she'd passed."

"I suppose that makes sense. Ye didna visit while ye were away?"

Broderick heaved in a chestful of air. "Nay. My family and I, weel, we werena close after my mother passed." He didn't want to talk about his family. "Do ye like flowers?"

She looked taken aback by his question. "I do."

"My mother's gardens are maintained even though she has passed. Mayhap when ye are feeling better, we can walk through them?" He'd love to escort her through the rows of flowers his mother had painstakingly planted, her arm looped into his. She probably barely reached his shoulders.

She'd surely feel petite in his arms. Now wasn't the time, but in the future, it could be so.

She smiled. "I'd like that verra much."

Broderick couldn't stop the wide smile from spreading across his face. He was happy she agreed.

Her eyes clouded over. She caught him looking at her and she sniffled but gave him a slight smile. "My mother loved flowers. We would often pick wildflowers from the forest. They always made my father sneeze, but not once did he ever complain. He loved the way they brightened my mother's eyes."

"Loved?" He caught the way she spoke of her parents in past tense.

Sadness crossed her face, and she bit her lower lip as if she were biding time to tamper her emotions before answering. "Aye. My mother was the one who told me to run to the woods during the attack. When our village was overrun with the invaders and our small home descended upon, my mother only thought of my safety. I saw her struck down by one of the monsters before I turned and ran for my life."

"Maggie, lass, I'm verra sorry for yer loss. Losing one loved one is hard enough. Losing both of yer parents in one quick moment is most difficult. Especially when the three of ye loved each other as much as ye did."

Maggie dropped her chin to her chest and swiped at a tear rolling down her cheek. "Thank ye," she whispered so low, he almost didn't hear her.

He softened his features, even though he wanted to coil in anger. But he knew that would frighten her and that was the last thing he wanted to do. "Ye can tell me anything, lass. Anything," he coaxed softly.

She nodded, her eyes searching his face and then finally, opened up to him.

~

MAGGIE'S HEART ACHED. Her chest felt heavy. And she felt herself saying the words that she hadn't planned on telling Broderick. But his coaxing was like a salve to her healing wounds and broken heart.

"They attacked on the darkest of nights. I was awakened by the screams of my friends and the smell of smoke." She sniffed and swiped at her nose. "I ran from the croft I'd grown up in. Knowing my parents no longer breathed."

"That attack. That's what ye were running from? The other night?"

She almost laughed. She wished that was all that happened. The deaths of her parents and friends were awful and she'd spent enough nights wishing she had died with them. "Nay. As I tried to escape, I was caught at the edge of the woods."

She paused. She could see the scene play out in her mind the way it had so many times since that night.

Broderick stiffened and she could see him clench his jaw, the veins in his neck straining.

"I was forced on his horse and we rode for what seemed liked forever before we arrived at the most ominous looking fortress. I hadn't seen it that night, but I did the day I was let go."

The laird was silent for a long moment, his face taut with anger. "How long were ye there?"

"I canna say honestly. I was kept in a windowless room."

His head snapped up. "'Tis why you like to feel the sun on yer skin."

"Aye."

"Did..." Broderick started.

Maggie could tell he was trying to tamp down his anger.

And even though she knew it wasn't aimed at her, her breath quickened.

"Did he..." Broderick started again, and once again let the question trail away.

"Aye," she cried, a huge sob wracking her body, paining her chest.

"That bastard!" Broderick swore with such vehemence, Maggie could see the power he held. But it didn't frighten her. She knew his anger wasn't directed at her, but at Diel. And she was grateful to have such a force on her side.

He softened his gaze when he looked at her, his face showing regret. "I'm sorry, lass. I didna mean to frighten ye. It's just," he ran his hands through his hair. "I canna imagine what ye endured and I'm verra sorry for that."

Maggie shook her head. "Ye didna scare me. Yer reaction matches my own."

Her words came out fierce, surprising herself. But she felt the same way. Diel was a bastard. A bastard that would pay.

Maggie inhaled in deeply and let out a slow breath.

"I like yer spirit, lass. But I fear I've overstayed my welcome. Which wasn't my intention. I shall take my leave. Ye needn't speak any more of that ordeal. And I feel like I keep repeating myself, but ye truly are safe here. I promise ye with everything I have that no harm will come to ye."

Mayhap Maggie was a fool, but she believed him. His promises struck her as genuine.

With her story of what happened out in the open, she felt a bit of weight lifted off her shoulders. "Thank ye. For every-thing ye've done for me."

A soft knock sounded and Orna poked her head into the room. "My lady, may I come in?" she asked quietly, concern furrowing her brows when her eyes met Maggie's.

"My laird? I apologize. I dinna mean to interrupt."

"'Tis nothing, Orna. We were just speaking of losses of

our past." She fixed her eyes on Broderick, pleading with him to say nothing further.

He nodded, but she could see that he was holding onto the anger. Broderick MacLeod was not one to let a wrong go unpunished. Maggie could see that.

But this wrong was hers to right. Diel was hers to deal with.

"I'll leave ye two alone." Broderick stood and gave her a slight bow.

"I look verra much forward to that walk, Laird Broderick."

He didn't correct her use of laird. Just bowed again and said, "As do I, Lady Maggie." Then he slipped out the door.

MAGGIE'S EYES followed Broderick as he left the room.

"Are ye and the laird making plans?" Orna pulled a bench to the chair where Maggie sat and patted her lap.

Maggie was unsure what she wanted.

"Let me see yer foot, my lady."

Maggie ducked her head to hide her embarrassment as she gingerly lifted her foot onto Orna's lap. With deceptively gentle hands, Orna slowly and carefully unwrapped the dressing covering the many cuts and scrapes on the bottoms of Maggie's feet.

"He asked me to walk through the gardens when I was feeling better," Maggie said regarding Orna's earlier question.

"Aye. His mother's gardens. She was very proud of them when she was here," she explained as she rubbed a salve on Maggie's foot that left her skin tingling.

"He mentioned that it was her favorite place."

"Aye, she spent a lot of time tending to them." She

finished wrapping Maggie's foot and gently placed it on the floor before lifting her other foot and repeating the process. "These are healing nicely. This balm will help yer feet heal quicker. I think one more poultice wrap will be all they need and ye will be able to walk normally again."

Maggie let out a sigh of satisfaction. "That would be nice. Thank ye. I dinna know how to thank ye for all ye've done for me. Everyone here has been so kind." She didn't know how she would repay Orna and Broderick and everyone else that had treated her with nothing but tenderness and care. But she would find a way.

"No need to thank me, my lady. Anyone would have done the same."

"If only that were true," Maggie said quietly.

The look of empathy on Orna's kind face held understanding of all she'd been through.

She stood and patted Maggie on the shoulder. "Ye're in good hands now. And ye're safe."

Alone in her room once again, she began to repeat the mantra that was fast becoming her driving force.

Diel's name. Diel's lands. Diel's castle.

They would all be razed to the ground.

CHAPTER 8

*B*roderick's hands itched for a fight. It had been too long since he'd practiced combat with his men. He missed the rush he got every time he bested an opponent.

He just needed the release physical activity offered to get his mind off everything that had happened over the past several days.

The lass. His father. His brother.

All three of them needed justice.

He followed the hoots and hollers of what sounded like men fighting and grinned.

To his delight, men sparred out in the yard. Paired up in teams of two, they practiced combat with swords, axes, and fists. The urge to join and spar with them was too strong to ignore.

He surveyed the men. All were of good height and brawny. Could one or two of them be the killers he sought? It was possible.

What was the name Alastair had mentioned? Liam. But he was no longer in the clan's guard. He worked for the blacksmith now. Mayhap he still liked to train.

He approached a couple of men who had just finished sword practice and were taking a respite, their chests heaving.

"My laird," they said in unison, each bowing slightly.

Broderick dipped his head in acknowledgment. "Are either of ye familiar with Liam?"

They raised their brows at his question and the taller one nodded his head, his long red hair falling into his eyes before he swept it back. "Aye. The bastard was stealing yer da's coin."

"So I've heard." He scanned the men that continued to train. "Is he here?"

"Nay. He's working with the blacksmith pounding iron in the village. He doesna come to the castle often."

That made sense. He probably wasn't accepted among the guard anymore. And Broderick was sure he'd lost all respect with the men he used to serve with.

"How about his acquaintances? Anyone still on the guard he was close to?"

The two men glanced at each other and then over to two men that were training bare-handed.

"Aye. Smitty. The blond fighting hand to hand over there. At least they were. I canna say if they still are since the fallout."

Broderick listened intently as the man talked. Observed his actions. He seemed honest and trustworthy. "What's yer name?"

"Declan, my laird."

"I appreciate the information, Declan. Carry on with yer practice."

"Aye, my laird."

Broderick was going to need some time to get used the sound of being addressed as laird. Every time someone said it, he expected his father to come rounding the corner.

He sauntered over to where Smitty was training bare-handed with another man and leaned against the wall, watching for a few minutes. The pair of fighters were good.

Broderick was better. The men may have been trained by Callum and Ewan, but Broderick had been trained by Alastair. And of the three, Alastair was the superior fighter.

Bare-handed was Broderick's specialty and his preferred way of fighting. Many a large purse had been won with the skills of his fists. Broderick broke into the pair. Smitty, the blond Declan had mentioned, was tall and broad shouldered. The other man, a bit shorter and stockier had dark hair that was matted to his face, damp with sweat from the exertion of the fight.

"Smitty, am I right?" Broderick eyed the man, concern clouding his reddened features.

"Aye."

"Let's spar."

The pair exchanged looks and the dark-haired man dipped his head in a slight bow and went to the outer circle to wait and left Smitty to fight Broderick.

The fighter looked pissed to miss out on a scuffle, but he'd be thankful for the reprieve once he saw the beatdown Broderick planned on giving the possible co-conspirator of his family's murders.

Bending at the waist, Broderick brought his hands up, urging the man, who looked to be similar in age, forward with a crook of his fingers. "Show me what ye've got."

Smitty smiled, no doubt thinking he was going to make a show to everyone and best the laird. He didn't know Broderick at all. The man lunged and Broderick easily side-stepped out of the way and kicked him in the arse on his way past. The crowd laughed and Smitty glared at them.

Broderick turned and waited for the man to charge again.

He didn't. Smitty approached slowly, methodically, fists clenched and raised at chest level.

"Ye know Liam?" Broderick asked.

That gave the man pause. Straightening, he dropped his arms. "Aye," he said, swiping at the sweat on his brow with the back of his hand.

Broderick moved to the side, circling the man. "How well?"

Smitty shrugged. "No' enough to ken he was stealing from the former laird if that's what ye're insinuating."

The answer surprised Broderick. Was the fighter saying that to clear the air, or was he trying to throw suspicion off himself?

It was too soon for Broderick to tell.

But Smitty was a thinker. Broderick respected that.

"Would ye have said something if ye did?"

"Of course." Smitty replied sharply.

Broderick studied the man's face, unsure if that were true or not. He bent, squaring his shoulders.

Smitty did the same. For a few moments, they stared at each other. Broderick waited, anticipating a charge.

He was right, Smitty dropped low and drove his head into Broderick's gut. He expected the move and brought his elbow down into the middle of the other man's back, then brought his knee up and cracked him in the face.

Smitty dropped to his knees with a huff.

Broderick walked back, giving the man some space to gather his wits about him. He leaned to the side and spat blood into the dirt, then wiped the back of his hand across his nose that was bleeding and starting to swell. After a few long moments, Smitty stood, fists up, eyes dark with anger, and planted his feet into a fighting stance to face Broderick once again.

Broderick allowed him to get in a punch. The hit landing

on his left jaw, barely phasing him. Broderick returned the favor and answered with his own punch to the jaw.

Smitty dropped like a rotting pile of timber. Out cold.

Mutters and cheers rose from the crowd that had gathered around to watch the new laird fight against one of their own. Whispers of respect rippled through them.

Broderick reveled in the cheers. He wanted more. That one fight was over way too quickly. He turned around, meeting all the eyes that stared back at him, looking for a worthy opponent.

Broderick MacLeod had grown up fighting. Fighting for everything he held dear. Fighting for those weaker than himself. Fighting for those in need.

He studied the men around him. Urged them forward with his hands. None advanced. No one wanted to take him on. Smitty started to rouse, his meaty hand coming up to rub his bearded jaw, now starting to swell as badly as his nose.

He sat up wonkily, not ready to attempt standing. He glared at Broderick, no doubt pissed to have been bested by the 'useless' son.

Broderick stuck out a hand. An offer to help the man up. Smitty seethed for another long moment, before ceding and clasping Broderick's hand and pulled himself up.

It would take some time, but one way or another he would prove to these men and himself that he could lead them. That he had the ability to do so and to keep the clan safe. Once he could prove that, he would gain their full respect.

The biggest thing that would help that along would be bringing Callum and Ewan's killer or killers to justice.

"Ye fight with passion. My father taught ye well."

"No' well enough, 'twould seem," Smitty mumbled as he opened and closed his mouth, no doubt trying to ease the stiffness beginning to form.

"I can see ye're a fine warrior. I apologize for taking things too far. I fear I let my emotions of recent events get the better of me."

"Aye, 'tis understandable, even if painful." Smitty smirked, the rest of the men joining in on the laughter.

Broderick could see the building blocks of trust growing, but he did feel sorry for Smitty. The statement wasn't a lie.

"Get back to it!" Broderick called out to the men and they scrambled back to their respective pairs, resuming their stances, and continuing their practice.

"No' ye," he stopped Smitty from rejoining the men. The fact that the man wanted to continue to train showed Broderick how strong and dedicated a warrior he was. "Ye dinna have to carry on."

The man lifted a blond brow, giving Broderick a defiant look. "Ye think I'd let a wee punch and a knee stop me from training?"

Broderick chuckled, liking Smitty's grit. "Weel, go on. When ye've finished, come find me. I'd like to discuss Liam some more."

"Aye, my laird." Smitty tilted his head in a slight nod and then ran full force into the middle of a pair of fighting men as if he hadn't just been out cold in the dirt minutes ago.

The castle wall caught Broderick's attention and his gaze fell upon the window of the room where Maggie was being tended to. He was thankful to Orna for her care and the compassion she was showing the lass.

He was anxious to see and talk with her some more. Broderick ignored the obvious meaning of how whenever he was away from her, he wanted to be near her. But also, as much as he wanted to know more about her attacker, pressing the lass would not be of benefit. The last thing he wanted to do was force her to talk before she was ready.

No matter how many advances they'd made so far in their

relationship. If that's what he could call what they were trying to build. Friendship?

Either way, he needed to wait until she was ready to give the information freely. The ordeal had been horrific for her. The last thing he wanted to do was make her relive it.

Whatever it was. Though he had a pretty good idea considering the snippets of information she'd given him so far.

Broderick would wait for her. For some things, he could be a very patient man.

Before seeing Maggie, he needed to clean up. He smelled like sweat and the yard. Not enticing for any lass. Not that he was trying to entice, well, mayhap he was, but either way, he didn't want to repulse her nonetheless.

A fresh pair of trews and tunic were called for. He'd make it quick though. He was anxious to see her and ask if she needed anything.

～

BRODERICK KNOCKED on Maggie's door and waited for her answer. When it came, he walked in and greeted her with a smile, pausing just inside the doorframe.

Every time he visited, her physical injuries healed just a little bit more, allowing more of her beauty to shine through. She was like a mystery package that was being revealed to him one small piece at a time.

"My lady, I hope all is well."

"Please, ye dinna need to call me lady. I'm of no such station." Her hand traveled to her slender neck, her fingers skimming her the skin as if they were trying to locate an item there. Mayhap she previously wore a necklace of some sort that she would twist when anxious. Mayhap it was habit.

He grinned. "I'll make ye a barter. If ye promise to stop

calling me laird, I'll promise to stop calling ye lady." He raised a brow in challenge.

She blessed him with a small laugh and the sound was a song to his ears. "But ye are deserving of the title."

"Only as of a few weeks ago. And I came onto it in an unexpected way. 'Tis something I havena grown accustomed to yet."

She nodded as if she understood.

"May I come in?"

Her eyes darted behind him. Was she wondering if he was alone? Or was she wondering if she should allow him in? Most likely the latter and he couldn't blame her one bit. He'd be weary if he were in her position as well.

She patted her plaited hair nervously. "I apologize. Please. It appears I've forgotten my manners."

He entered the room but left the door open behind him and sat on the bench furthest away from her to allow her space. Broderick didn't want Maggie to be intimidated by him.

Once again, she was seated near the window, enjoying the warmth of the sun on her ivory skin. The rays danced off her honey-colored tresses, making bands of gold appear.

"I'd say ye've had a lot on yer mind. I just wanted to see how ye fare. Have ye supped yet?"

"I feel better as each hour passes. Thank ye." Her hands were in her lap, and she kept squeezing the tips of her fingers, starting with her pinky and moving through her thumb before starting the sequence over again.

"I'm glad to hear you say that. 'Tis great news." He sounded like an oaf. There were so many things he wanted to say to her, but he held back. She didn't need to be burdened with his questions. She would reveal what she wanted to in due time. It wasn't his place to push her. He needed to keep his patience.

"Are ye hungry?" he asked, steering her to a safe topic of conversation. Food. One of his favorites.

"I havena eaten yet," she said quietly. "I'm no' saying Orna hasna been seeing to my needs." She rushed to add as if she were worried of getting Orna into trouble. "She has. More than I deserve. She's been naught but helpful and caring. Last time she came in, she did ask if I needed sustenance and I didna."

"And now?" He found it endearing that she wanted to ensure he knew Orna hadn't been ignoring her. The thought never crossed his mind. She was like a mother hen over him when he was young. He knew she was the same with Maggie. Mayhap more so considering everything the lass had been through.

Maggie gave him a shy smile and pinched her fingers together.

He noted the skin was healing nicely. The scrapes and cuts were now thin lines, no longer red and swollen.

"Mayhap a wee bit." Pink tinged her cheeks.

"Say no more. I'll be right back."

"Ye dinna need to fret, my—Broderick. I'll be fine 'til the morn."

"Nonsense. I'll return shortly."

In the kitchens Broderick ignored the complaints from the women working there and grabbed a trencher. Surveying the fare laid out on the tables, he chose what he thought Maggie would enjoy—a chunk of bread, braised hare, mushroom pasties, and an onion tart. He looked at the trencher and contemplated if that would be enough. The lass must be starving with all the healing her body was going through.

He added some roast fowl and some vegetables. He paused again. Mayhap something sweet. Shrugging, he added a custard tart before snatching a mug and a pitcher of ale.

Happy with what he'd chosen, he carefully balanced

everything in his arms as he made his way back to Maggie's room, passing Orna on the way.

"Where are ye going with all that?"

"I'm bringing Maggie her evening meal."

Orna's eyes widened. "The lass said she wasna hungry when I last checked in on her."

"Weel, now she is." He cocked his head to the side. "A wee bit hungry, that is."

"Ye've got enough food there for three men."

"She's healing. She needs all the sustenance she can get."

Orna waved him off with a laugh. "As ye will, my laird," and continued walking.

With his hands full, he tapped the toe of his boot on Maggie's door and managed to open the door without dropping any of the items he'd brought.

Maggie looked up, her blue eyes round in surprise. She made a move to get up as if to help him.

"Lass, please. Stay seated."

She relaxed back into her chair and he set everything on the table. "I wasna sure what yer preference was, so I brought ye a variety," he grinned sheepishly.

"'Tis too much," she insisted as she studied the food he'd chosen for her.

She didn't say it, but she looked yearningly at the food. How hungry must she be? Broderick feared that she hadn't eaten well for a while before coming to Straik. Her health hadn't been a priority in her previous circumstances. That much was obvious.

Maggie was still too thin. It would do her good to get some meat on her bones.

He arranged the fare on the table and poured some ale and handed her the mug.

She took a small sip before setting it on the small table near the chair.

"Ye know, my brother and I used to play in this room as young lads." He carefully stepped around her to give her space and not frighten her with his close proximity and placed the trencher on the nearby table so she could easily reach it, then stepped back. "Before the worries and responsibilities of life interfered."

She watched him for a moment, while gingerly picking up the tart and taking a small bite. She closed her eyes and savored the rich taste and Broderick couldn't help but be happy that he chose something she enjoyed. She opened her eyes and her gaze fell to the wall near the bed.

"Are those yer etchings over there?"

He followed her gaze, surprised the carvings, though faint, were still there. "Aye. We would both take turns scratching different things into the stone. But that was before," he paused. Broderick didn't need to burden Maggie with his unhappy childhood. She'd seen enough sadness lately. He gave her a smile. "Those were happy times."

He watched her as she took a bit of braised hare, and a moan of satisfaction escaped her lips.

As inappropriate as it was, he had never wanted to be a rabbit so much.

"I, um," Broderick cleared his throat. "I hope the food is to yer liking."

"'Tis verra delicious. It has been a long time since I've had such a meal."

He nodded in understanding but didn't press her further. He felt a sense of pride knowing that he was able to offer her something that she so enjoyed.

"I'm glad to be the one to provide it to ye, lass. Ye deserve delicious food aplenty."

She didn't speak on his statement. Instead, she change the subject. "Tell me about yer brother. He was older than ye, aye?"

Broderick pursed his lips and nodded. "Aye. Being the firstborn son, yer fate is written as soon as ye breathe yer first breath. Such as it was with Ewan. Our father made sure my brother and I knew from a young age that Ewan will lead the clan when the time came."

Maggie slowly chewed the bite of mushroom pasty she'd just taken, digesting both the food and what he'd just told her. "But that time never came?"

"Nay. Someone made sure of it."

"The fates have an odd way of working sometimes."

Her statement brought the reality back to Broderick that the fates had been just as cruel, if not even more so to Maggie.

"They do."

"Are ye going to find who did it?" Maggie asked quietly, her voice barely above a whisper.

"The one responsible for the deaths of my father and brother?"

Maggie nodded.

"Aye. And they will pay."

A fire burned in Maggie's blue eyes. "I can understand that. People who do such deeds should meet their maker," she stated fiercely.

That warrior spirit was strong in the lass. He imagined she'd be a force to reckon with once she was healed fully.

And he couldn't wait to see it. He'd be by her side to offer her any support she might need. Though he got the feeling Maggie of unknown surname wanted to handle this fight on her own.

He admired that spark in her and he'd work to help her nurture the flame, not tamp it down to embers and ash.

~

THE NEXT SEVERAL days were a whirlwind of healing for both Maggie's body and heart.

She was now able to move freely about her room without pain now that her body had recovered from most of the injuries inflicted by Diel. All the swelling had gone away, and the coloring of her bruises had faded to a dull yellow.

Broderick made sure to visit her a few times a day and she'd grown to really enjoy their time together.

Today she sat in the chair, eagerly awaiting his visit for their much-anticipated walk in his mother's gardens. He'd mentioned the walk days ago, but she hadn't felt up to it until now.

She stood and looked out the window. The sky was gray, and the days were growing colder. Soon, snow would cover the ground.

Maggie knew she would need to make the decision on when to leave Straik to track down Diel.

With each visit from Broderick the pull to stay grew stronger, but she had to fight it. She couldn't stay. As safe as she felt here, it wasn't her home. She didn't have a home anymore. But the more she stayed, the more she could see Straik as her home. The staff. The clan and townspeople she'd met. Orna.

Broderick.

All of them reminded her of family which flooded her with mixed emotions. She was happy to find people so caring and loving, but it also made her miss her parents and friends who had died at Diel's cruel hands. Every time she thought of them it was like Diel kicking her in the stomach all over again. It would be a while before she could get the images of their broken bodies out of her mind and their screams out of her ears.

It would be a relief when she would finally be able to think of only the happy times.

Everyone here was making that transition easier and she was grateful to them all. She was forever in their debt.

Mayhap when the time came when she was fully healed and able to leave Broderick would make her go. Just the thought was laughable. She was quite sure that the laird was as enamored with her as she was him.

Though she couldn't possible see why.

But that didn't matter. What mattered was making sure that Diel paid for all he'd done. Maggie only hoped that the beast hadn't found another lass to mistreat in the time since he'd let her go. And for her to be able to track him down, she would need to leave Straik and everyone here behind.

Her head snapped to the door at the sound of a sharp knock. She ran her damp palms on skirt. Why was she nervous? She had no reason to be.

Broderick greeted her with a wide smile, his eyes dancing in delight. "Ye look lovely, lass."

Her cheeks grew warm at the compliment. "Thank ye."

"Are ye ready? I've brought ye this." He entered the room and handed her a beautiful emerald green hooded cloak. "The weather has turned cold and I dinna want ye catching a chill while we are out."

She ran her fingers over the soft material. She'd never owned anything so nice.

"May I?" His deep voice slid down her spine like warm honey.

Maggie was speechless. She nodded and Broderick took the garment from her hands and unfurled it, placing it around her shoulders.

Maggie tied the ribbons at her neck, she could already feel its warmth heating her skin. "'Tis verra lovely, ye shouldna have."

"'Twas my pleasure. I dinna want ye to be cold whilst we

walk." He held out his arm for her to take, waiting patiently when she didn't accept it right away.

It would be the first time she touched him. She pushed the dark thoughts of Diel out of her mind. He had no place in this moment.

Could Broderick sense her nerves? Her hesitation. He didn't push her in anyway and remained the perfect gentleman.

Tentatively, she reached out, her fingers skimming the linen sleeve of his tunic. Maggie wasn't sure what she expected to happen, but nothing did. At her touch, Broderick didn't suddenly lunge at her. Just the opposite, he stood stock still, allowing her to set the pace.

He had the countenance of her father, who had always treated her mother with love and respect. Maggie too. If times were different and her father were still alive, she believed they would get on well. They both shared the same fierce protective nature.

Sliding her arm fully into the crook of his elbow, Maggie smiled at Broderick letting him know she was ready. She could feel the heat radiating from his skin. She couldn't deny the pleasant ribbon circling up her arm.

"We can go as slow as ye like, lass. And when ye want to stop, ye let me know."

She nodded, took a deep breath, inhaling the spicy, woodsy scent that was uniquely Broderick and stepped out of her room.

Castle-goers bowed at them as they passed, genuine smiles brightened their faces as they greeted them. A sense of home filled Maggie. Something she hadn't felt in a long time.

And something she didn't need to feel. Seeing Straik as her home would only make it harder for her when the time came to leave.

CHAPTER 9

The sun that shone through Maggie's chamber window earlier was now obscured by fluffy gray clouds that filled the sky and chilled the air.

She shivered and clasped the cape tighter around her shoulders.

"Are ye cold? We can go back inside." Broderick's voice was laced with concern.

"Nay, I'm fine." She wouldn't admit that she was cold. Not when she could be outside enjoying the fresh air.

And assessing her surroundings. That was crucial information she would need in her quest to find Diel.

Pausing, she looked around. The courtyard was thrumming with life. Wee ones chased each other around, their belly giggles echoing off the castle walls. Men trained, the clang of swords as they practiced sharp in Maggie's ears. Women carried baskets filled with vegetables and herbs made their way inside. Probably getting ready to start the evening meal.

Everyone looked happy and content. No one leered or shouted vile things at her. It was so different than the time

Diel had moved her from one dark room to another. His men hollered the most disgusting things at her as she passed. But she didn't want to sully Straik with memories of that other castle. They were clearly two different places with two very different men leading them.

Straik Castle loomed large and tall, casting a shadow over the yard that added to the chill in the air. But unlike the dark castle Diel had kept her in, Straik was bright and not foreboding in the least.

The mere sight of it didn't send shivers down her spine.

She felt Broderick's eyes studying her, but when she looked at him, he averted his gaze, suddenly very interested in the surrounding trees.

The trees. Were those the woods Broderick had found her in? Her breath quickened. Could Diel be close?

"Are ye alright, lass?"

Heat filled her cheeks, and she dipped her head. He was very observant. Without realizing it, she'd stiffened at the thought of Diel.

"Aye. I'm sorry. A brief memory of the past. 'Tis gone now," she lied.

His brows furrowed with concern, but he didn't press her for more information.

Maggie knew now that Broderick wouldn't insist she tell him what was filling her mind. He allowed her the time she needed. She was thankful for that.

They continued on and her mind calmed. It had taken them almost a full day's ride to get from where he found her to the castle from what she'd been told, so these weren't the same woods.

An arched trellis, covered with ivy, came into view. The entrance to the garden.

"I haven't spent much time here since my mother passed," Broderick broke the silence. "Even before I left. The first few days after she died, you couldna pry me out of this space. But then..." His voice trailed off and his statement hung unfinished in the crisp air between them.

She could hear the pain in his voice. Sense it in the tensing of the muscles of his forearm. She didn't know his history, but she knew that he'd suffered his own trials and tribulations.

And her heart ached for him. She caught herself in her thoughts. The two of them had a lot in common when it came to their families. They'd both lost those they'd loved dearly.

Even though his past was sad, Maggie couldn't hold her tongue and stop herself from asking. "How did yer mother pass?"

Broderick glanced up at the sky, squinted his eyes and clenched his jaw.

She waited, not sure if he was willing to let her glimpse into his past.

"I was eight when my mother died from a festering wound. She'd fallen when my father and brother were gone. I tried to do everything I could to help her, but couldna."

"Ye were just a child."

"I was. In my father's eyes that didna matter." He pushed his hand through his hair and blew out a breath. "I bore my father's wrath from that day forward even more so than afore."

"How so?" She bit her lip. "If ye dinna mind me asking." She felt the muscle in his arm jump.

Broderick looked her in the eyes and gave her a small smile. "My father was two different people. One for his clan and one for his family." He ducked under the trellis as they passed to avoid hitting his head.

They continued on the path around the outside of the garden, surrounded by greenery on both sides as they walked. It enveloped them and acted as a natural tunnel. The air was even cooler here, away from the bit of warmth the faded sun offered.

Maggie waited for Broderick to speak. She got the feeling this wasn't a subject he spoke of often.

He licked his lips and let out a small sigh. "The clan adored my father. He was well respected by them."

She could see that. In the time she'd been here, she didn't think anyone had ever said anything untoward about the previous laird. And she remembered her father had thought highly of him as well.

"At home, with my mother and I, he was a completely different person He ruled the family with a heavy fist and used it often. The night my father came home after learning my mother had passed, he beat me so severely, I still bear those scars today."

Maggie brought he hand to her mouth to cover her gasp. "Why? Ye couldna have saved her. Ye must have done everything ye possibly could."

"Aye. It wasna enough and she still passed. But Callum, my father, always blamed me."

Maggie stopped walking and placed her hand on Broderick's shoulder. "I'm verra sorry ye were treated in such a fashion. Parents are supposed to protect us. No' the opposite."

For a brief moment, Broderick closed his eyes and placed his hand on top of hers. The gesture warmed her fingers, and she found she rather liked the action. When he pulled his hand away, the warmth disappeared and she folded her hands together in front of her, wrapping them in the cloak.

"I agree with ye, lass. And it is something I've sworn to do when I have children of my own."

The thought of Broderick's wee ones running around the courtyard and castle halls and him cheerfully chasing them, all with huge smiles plastered on their faces flooded Maggie's mind. She wanted that for him. He'd be a wonderful father. The cruel family legacy of his father would end with Broderick.

"Here, be careful." He held out his hand for her to take so she could step over a fallen tree. It wasn't a large tree, but big enough where she might trip if she tried stepping over it on her own.

She placed her hand in his and as he wrapped his fingers around hers, she again reveled in the feeling of his touch.

"Thank ye." She gave him a smile and hoped he could see how genuinely thankful she truly was to him.

Once again, the connection ended too quickly, and she felt the absence of his touch as they moved forward along the path.

"I can see that the gardens haven't been cared for quite like they should. It saddens me to see this."

"If ye dinna mind I would like to offer to help clean the gardens up? It's something I used to do with my mother and I enjoyed it."

"That's verra kind of ye. But I couldna ask ye to do such a thing. I can have some of the castle staff work in here. I'm sure there must be some assigned to do so. The gardens haven't been completely neglected."

"I really would like to help. Being outside helps cleanse my soul. And I enjoy working with my hands."

Broderick stopped in front of her and took her hands into his, his calloused fingers running over hers. Each movement sending a jolt of fire up her arms.

He lifted her hand to his mouth and placed his lips on the skin in a gentle kiss. The gesture was so light, if she hadn't seen him do it, she might not have believed it happened.

How could such a large warrior be so gentle?

"I'm sorry, lass. I couldna help myself. The moment seemed right to call for such an action."

"Dinna apologize. I'd be lying if I said I didna enjoy it."

Broderick beamed. His wide smile brightening his eyes. "Then let's continue," he held out his hand. "May I?"

Maggie bent her head back to look him in the eye and then glanced down at his outstretched hand before returning his smile and placing her hand in his. He curled is fingers around her hand, which felt so small enveloped in his.

She was feeling things she had never felt before. Deep down. Down in her belly. A mass of butterflies flew about.

Hand in hand they walked through the garden. Broderick showed Maggie where flowers would bloom in the spring. The spot that once summer came, a rainbow of colors would flourish to life and transform the garden into a spectacular display of vibrance.

He spoke as if she would still be here during those times. And she reveled in the fact that maybe she would be.

But she also had to find Diel. She had to stop him before he could hurt anyone else. Because only then could she ever truly rest and find happiness. He had to pay for what he'd done.

His day of reckoning would come, and it would be delivered by the last person he ever thought he would see again.

Diel thought she was dead.

She couldn't wait to see his surprise when she arrived to exact her revenge.

CHAPTER 10

*B*roderick wasn't one to take part in such trivial gestures, but as he strode alongside Maggie, her small hand curled snugly into his, he realized he didn't want to be anywhere else.

After his mother died and he'd left Straik, whenever he thought of the garden, a deep sadness would overcome him, but right now, in this moment, that melancholy was melting away, bit by bit.

Memories of his beautiful mother enjoying the garden were now being added to with the bonny lass by his side.

He shook his head. Alastair would be thrilled if he knew the thoughts that were currently running through his mind. The man would be downright giddy.

"Are ye alright?" Maggie's small voice broke into his thoughts, and he focused on her. She studied him intently. Her sky blue eyes searching his face for an answer.

Broderick squeezed her fingers. "Aye. 'Tis a pleasure showing ye my mother's garden and I'm delighted to see ye also enjoy it."

"'Tis really a charming space. I can see why yer mother loved to spend her time here. 'Tis so tranquil."

"I wish she were still here to partake of it. However, she's in a more peaceful place now, not having to feel the wrath of Callum."

Maggie nodded but stayed silent.

"Come on. I want to show ye something."

Wanting to lighten the mood, Broderick grasped her hand a little tighter and quickened their pace as he led her to the far corner of the gardens, towards his mother's favorite area. As they got closer, Broderick slid behind Maggie.

"Do ye trust me, lass?" He asked, his mouth close to her ear.

She turned and met his eyes and he held his breath, waiting for her answer. He wanted her trust. It surprised him how much he wanted it.

After a few long moments of Maggie searching his face, she slowly nodded. "Aye, I do trust ye."

His grin was so big he could feel it splitting his face. "Turn around." He said gently. When she did, he brought his hands up to shield her eyes.

A wee squeak escaped her lips, and she brought her hands up and wrapped her slim fingers around his wrists.

A deep chuckle rumbled up through his chest. "I dinna want ye to see it until ye are right in front of it."

"See what?"

"Ye'll see. Step straight in front of ye."

"But I canna see a thing." Maggie's voice wasn't strained or filled with worry. There was a singsong lilt to her statement and that made him happier than he had been in a long time.

"I promise I willna let ye bump into anything."

"I'm trusting ye as ye asked," she said as she began to move forward.

Broderick kept his hands in place as he watched the path to ensure she didn't stumble over any obstacles. Maggie's safety was his utmost priority. "I thank ye for that, Maggie."

Maggie.

He loved saying her name. Loved the way it played at the back of his throat.

"Alright, slow down. Almost there. Just a few more steps."

"One, two, three." Maggie counted out the steps and then stopped. "Are we there? Is this the spot?"

"Perfect."

Broderick looked to the stone room that stood before them. Built into the corner of the wall surrounding the castle, it was his mother's favorite place to pass her time. She would spend hours here. Drying herbs that grew in the gardens. Drying flowers to add to cleansing bars and salves.

Most wives loved needlepoint and embroidery. But not Elspeth. Nay, she loved being outdoors. It didn't matter the climate. Whenever he couldn't find his mother, he just needed to come out to this room where he would most certainly find her.

"Ready?"

Doubt suddenly seeped into his mind, and he swallowed a lump the size of a neep in his throat. Broderick was nervous at what Maggie's reaction was going to be. Maybe she wouldn't like this space as much as he thought. Maybe he's somehow conveying his own feelings for his mother onto Maggie.

"I am!" She exclaimed. Her fingers pulled at his wrists, trying to get him to uncover her eyes.

"Alright," he pulled his hands away and stepped back, waiting anxiously for her reaction and hoping it would be as he expected.

"'Tis a room."

"Aye," Broderick stepped around her. "But no' just any

room." Stepping forward he grasped the handle and pushed open the door. The familiar smell of peat and damp stone assaulted his senses and reminded him of childhood days spent watching his mother work. The room was dark, and he searched for a torch to light the space.

As the area around them lit up, he watched Maggie's face as she stepped forward and took it all in. Her mouth formed a little 'O' of awe, and he couldn't stop the smile that spread across his face. That was the exact reaction he'd hoped for.

She wandered around the room, trailing her fingers along the dusty tabletops as she studied the shelves holding jars and pots that his father had hung at his mother's request.

Broderick remembered the day and looking back on it now he was surprised his father did such a task for her. It wasn't often Callum afforded anything to Elspeth. He must have been feeling especially generous that day. He hated to think how she may have paid for it later that night once Callum's generosity had worn away.

"What is this place?" Maggie asked. "I know it's for the gardens, but my heavens, 'tis verra grand. My mother would have cherished such a space where she could dry her herbs instead of inside our small cottage."

Maggie's last line felt like a punch to the gut. Her life before he'd found her couldn't have been easy. He was happy he could offer her comfort now.

And in the future.

"My mother loved it as well. She spent hours in this room doing exactly that. When she wasn't running after my brother and I, that is."

Their eyes met and they remained silent for a few moments, as if each could read the other's mind. The connection he felt for this lass that he had only known a short time was foreign to Broderick.

He hadn't had many relationships in the past. His work

kept him too busy for that and even the thought of having a wife—and God forbid kids—while he was out running missions for the Amadán didn't sound like the ideal family. He would never be home. That wasn't the type of family life he wanted, nor did he want to subject his family to that type of life.

But he was laird now.

His missions would be coming to an end with the responsibilities that came with his new title.

And he would need an heir.

It would be expected of him to carry on the clan's glory.

He studied Maggie as she lifted a mortar and pestle and weighed the stone in her hand. Its heft was significant. He remembered when he used to hand it to his mother at her request.

"This is beautiful." The stone of the pestle had been worn smooth and Maggie turned it over in her hand.

"Thank ye. My mother used it often."

"We had a wooden one. My father had carved it himself." Her face clouded. "I'm sure it was lost in the fire when our village was..."

She let the sentence hang in the air unfinished.

"Would ye go back?"

Maggie snapped her gaze to his, biting her lower lip so hard, the pink turned to white, and shook her head. "Nay. I want to remember my village as it was before the attack. I've done my best to forget the images I saw that night. The sounds I heard. I only want the memories of happy times. Going back would destroy my most precious memories."

Broderick nodded. "I can understand that." He leaned against the doorframe as she continued to explore, opening the smalls drawers in the chest, picking up different dried plants that were still on the desk. He wouldn't think they were from his mother, they would have long ago, withered into dust. But he didn't think anyone was using this room either. Maybe someone from the kitchens had entered at some point.

The fireplace was clear of ashes. It was apparent that it hadn't been lit in quite some time. He found it odd that someone had come here and cleaned out the fireplace but left the plants.

"I'm sorry." She clasped her hands in front of her. "I'm overstepping my boundaries. My mother always said I was a curious one."

"Dinna apologize, lass. I brought ye here for this verra reason. I want ye to spend as much time in here as ye want. 'Twould be a shame for it to continue to go unused." He smiled. "I hope ye find it as much of a place for healing as my mother did."

MAGGIE WAS at a loss for words. The trust Broderick was putting on her was endearing. His willingness to share his mother's most precious spot with her and allow her to come here as she pleased was kindness on a level she hadn't experienced in a long time.

The room smelled musty from being closed for such a long time, but a day or two with the door open and a roaring fire would take care of that. Once she cleaned and dusted the tables and shelves, it would look like it had never been left abandoned for an extended period of time.

She glanced at Broderick and found that he was watching her intently. "What?"

His face lit up with a broad smile, brightening his blue eyes. "Ye look like ye are concocting a plan for this room. Ye look," he paused, "happy."

Maggie nodded. She couldn't deny it. She was happy. "I

am." Though she needed to remember, this wasn't her home. Straik belonged to Broderick, and she couldn't stay. If she did, she'd never find Diel and make him pay for what he'd done.

"I'm glad. Ye can spend as much time here as ye'd like. Whatever supplies ye may need, just tell me."

"That's verra kind of ye. Thank ye."

He clasped his hands and rubbed them briskly together. "First thing ye'll need is a fire, I'll make sure one gets started when ye are ready to come out here, but right now, the cold is moving in."

Maggie had been too enthralled by the space to even notice, but now that Broderick mentioned it, her fingertips felt like ice.

"Let's head inside and I'll see if I can wrangle some hot stew from Annag."

"That sounds divine." She dipped her head shyly. He studied her with such intensity, she felt her cheeks flush, despite the chilled air. She accepted his proffered elbow, and they made their way back through the gardens to the Great Hall, where Broderick led her to the dais where the laird always sat.

He pulled out the chair to the right of his so she could take a seat.

She looked around nervously. No one seemed to be paying them any attention, but she still didn't feel right taking a seat of such importance.

"I really shouldna," Maggie shook her head.

"Nonsense. Ye are my guest, and I willnae have ye sitting in any other place. Please," he waved a hand at the seat, offering it to her once again.

Maggie drew in a breath and blew it out in a huff. "If ye insist."

"Aye, I do." He winked at her, and she couldn't help but laugh. She gathered her skirts and took a seat.

Broderick took his place beside her, and Maggie wondered if this is what it was like to be the lady of the castle. Maids quickly appeared with mugs of ale and set them on the table in front of them.

"Is the rabbit stew ready?" Broderick asked.

"I will ask, my laird," she answered and disappeared down the hall that led to the kitchens.

Broderick bent his head toward Maggie and whispered, "If we listen verra carefully, we will most certainly hear Annag cursing me." His voice was light, and his eyes twinkled.

Maggie giggled and hiccup escaped her throat. She brought her hand to her mouth and mumbled and apology.

With a laugh, Broderick patted her on the back gently. "Dinna apologize. 'Tis a natural reflex."

His fingers lingered on her back, the heat of his hand seeped through her cloak.

He appeared to catch himself and dropped his arm. "'Twould seem I am the one who should apologize now."

Maggie turned in her chair and reached out for him. "Nay." She wrapped her fingers around his very large hand and quite liked the feeling. "If I minded ye touching me, I would have said so."

That was the truth. She enjoyed his touch. She wasn't scared of him when his fingers glanced over her back or shoulder. She didn't cringe in fear when he gazed at her. Just the opposite. Her insides fluttered in a most intriguing way.

And she quite liked it.

Broderick beamed. "Are ye warming up, lass? Shall I take yer cloak?"

She stood and untied the ribbons at her neck, and he

slipped the cloak off her shoulders. There was something intimate about the gesture and her heart jumped a beat.

A maid stepped forward and took the cloak from Broderick's hands. "I will return this to yer room, my lady."

"Thank ye," Maggie said quietly, but her mind was on what had just occurred. It wandered some more, and she wondered what it would feel like for Broderick to slide her dress off like that. She swallowed the lump in her throat. She shouldn't be thinking of such thoughts. It was improper.

Even if Broderick MacLeod was the most handsome man she'd ever seen.

CHAPTER 11

*B*roderick was poring over Straik's books when Alastair knocked firmly to enter.

"My laird."

Broderick lifted a brow in his mentor's direction and went back to reading.

"Ye ken I need to follow protocol?"

"Aye. But it doesna mean I need to like it."

Alastair chuckled. "I willna argue with ye on that point." He closed the door behind him and took a seat in the chair across from Broderick's desk. "I've news of Duff."

Broderick sighed. His childhood nemesis was not who he wanted to be thinking about right now. Or ever, really. But some things he couldn't ignore. No matter how much he wanted to. "Is he returning to Straik?"

"It seems to be so. He and his crew have been spotted traveling this way."

Closing the accounts book he was studying, Broderick swiped his hand through his hair and clenched his jaw. "I suppose it was too much to expect that he would stay away once he learned I came back to claim Straik."

"Aye. The bastard thought Straik would be his once your father passed and if anything ever happened to Ewan."

He narrowed his eyes. "Do ye think…" Broderick let the question trail off his tongue. Duff was a bastard, but even he didn't think the bastard was capable of such a betrayal.

"Nay." Alastair shook his head. "I dinna, but we can keep a close eye on him and his men when they arrive. 'Tis something we may want to do anyway."

"Ye dinna trust him?" Broderick was surprised considering he'd spent many years living with Duff and had watched him grow up. But he had a mean streak in him that ran deeper than the loch and Broderick only imagined that streak had gotten worse as the years wore on.

"He didna expect ye to return." Alastair pierced him with a fierce gaze. "Ever."

"Then he underestimated my duty to my clan."

Alastair laughed. "Hell, I underestimated ye. I wasna sure ye would return home when I sent the missive."

"Ye've known me all my life."

"Which is why I didna think ye'd return. Ye are a good man, Broderick. But ye are stubborn and set in yer ways. Ye like no' being held to one place."

Alastair wasn't wrong. He liked to travel around the lands. The Amadán missions allowed him to do just that. He only had to worry about himself. Not family. Not clansmen. Just himself. But his sense of duty was strong. And he couldn't let the MacLeod fall into Duff's wretched hands. He'd drive them into the ground and his people would be treated horribly. That wouldn't happen as long as he had breath in his body.

"True," he finally answered. "But Duff is a bastard. The MacLeod aren't his people, no matter how much he might want to claim them. If he wants a clan to run, he can go back home to the Campbell."

Alastair nodded. "Ye've always had a strong sense of duty, Broderick. That will get ye far in life."

Broderick didn't miss that he'd said his name instead of calling him laird. "I dinna ken about that. It seems I've just come full circle and am right back where I started." He stood and pushed aside the tapestry to peer outside. "Make sure the men keeping watch at the edge of the lands know Duff and his men will be arriving soon. They should be at full attention. In the odd chance that Duff is planning something, they should be aware and ready."

Alastair pushed off the chair and ambled toward the door. "Aye. The men will be ready."

Alone in the room once again, Broderick pushed the thoughts of Duff out of his mind. Every time he thought of the bastard, he saw red. He was transported back to that time when they were young and Callum had chosen Duff over his own flesh and blood.

But in the end, it was all for naught. No matter what Duff thought was rightfully his. Without the MacLeod name to back him, he had no claim to Straik.

Broderick would ensure that fact remained true.

STRAIK HAD BEEN BUSTLING all day. Castlefolk running to and fro preparing the Great Hall for the much anticipated *cèilidh* that Broderick announced a few days earlier. The cooks in the kitchen, under Annag's watchful eye, carefully prepared a fare fit for the king.

As Maggie walked the halls, that's all anyone was talking about. Excited voices chattering about the bards that were invited, the fiddlers and pipers that will be playing. Young maidens whispered about which lads they hoped to dance with.

It was sweet watching them divulge their young love interests in hushed voices. Maggie couldn't help but smile whenever she happened to overhear a conversation.

She'd gone to the kitchens to ask Annag if she could help in any way, but the woman pushed her out of the kitchen quickly, refusing any offerings of assistance Maggie offered.

So now, she just wandered the halls and the main rooms and watched as it all came together. Tapestries in the Great Hall were taken down and beaten until they were dust-free and the colors bright before being hung back up. New rushes were spread on the floor after they'd been swept clean. The tables were rearranged to make room for dancing.

"My lady."

Maggie turned at the sound of Una's voice. Her maid was quickly walking towards her, a bundle of folded cloth in her arms.

Maggie stopped and waited for Una to catch up to her. "What is it?" She asked, as the maid drew near.

"Laird MacLeod sent this for ye." She paused in front of Maggie and handed her the bundle.

"What is it?"

Una grinned and leaned in close. "I believe the laird ordered a gown from the tailor for ye for tonight's *cèilidh*. I'd say he has taken a fancy to ye."

Maggie's cheeks heated. "I think he's just being kind." But secretly, her stomach did a tumble at the thought of Broderick thinking of her intimately.

"Let's go get ye ready, my lady. The time will be here before we know it."

In Maggie's room, she untied the bundle and unfurled the gown tucked inside. Una stepped forward and shook out the piece.

They both sucked in a breath at the same time. Made of

the softest wool, it was the finest piece of clothing that Maggie had ever owned.

"My lady," Una whispered. "Ye are going to draw the eye of everyone in attendance."

Maggie grimaced. "I hope no'." She collapsed on the bed and covered her eyes with her arm. She didn't want everyone's attention. Or anyone's attention.

Well, mayhap *one* person's attention.

She could hear Una moving about the room. No doubt readying the items to help Maggie dress and fix her hair. Sitting up, her eyes landed on the dress that Una had draped over one of the chairs.

It was beautiful and she was sure Broderick had spent a fortune having the dress made. To know that he cared for her so much to make such a grand gesture, along with everything else he'd done for her so far Maggie feared once again that she could never repay him.

He'd told her before that repayment wasn't necessary, but it didn't feel right to take so much and not offer anything in return.

Somehow, some way, Maggie would repay her debts. Even if it took her years to do so.

THE SOUND of fiddles and boots stomping on the floor filled the air as Maggie descended the stairs. Raucous laughter could be heard as she got closer to the Great Hall. She paused outside the entrance and waved her hands in front of her to dry her damp palms.

She didn't know why she was so nervous. She and Broderick had spent hours together. Everyone in the castle had seen them together. Their stolen glances. They're subtle touches.

Tucking a loose curl behind her ear, Maggie sucked in a deep breath and stepped into the hall.

She scanned the crowd, searching for Broderick and found him sitting at a table speaking with Alastair and another man she didn't recognize. Broderick's knee bounced to the beat of the jig that was playing. He looked up and his eyes darkened before he abruptly stood and headed her way.

Her heart skipped a beat or two and her pulse quickened. He looked very handsome in his belted plaid and linen shirt. As he drew near, a wide smile on his face, his scent enveloped her. Pine and peat. It would forever be embedded in her memory.

"Lass," Broderick dipped his head and whispered close to her ear. "Ye look bonny."

His deep voice rumbled over her, and she smiled shyly before dipping into a small curtsy. "Thank ye. And many thanks for the beautiful dress. 'Tis too much."

He straightened and swept his gaze over her. "Nay, lass. 'Tis no' enough."

Maggie got the feeling there was more he wanted to say, but he didn't continue. She wished he would realize he'd done so much for her already.

"Would ye like a drink?"

"Aye."

He clasped her hand and drew her further in the hall, moving toward the table she had spotted him at earlier. As they passed, clansmen raised their cups to them in salute. The ale seemed to be flowing at an unending pace and everyone was enjoying the night.

Alastair and the other man stood as they approached.

"My lady, good eve. Ye look lovely."

"Thank ye, Alastair. Ye look quite dashing yerself." A slight pink tinged his cheeks and Maggie ducked her head to hide her smile.

"Maggie, this is Doughall Munro. A friend of mine and Alastair's who's here for a visit."

Doughall, who was even taller than Broderick, bowed deeply at the introduction. "'Tis a pleasure to make yer acquaintance, my lady. I've heard naught but good things."

Maggie raised her brows, surprised that the man had known about her at all. "'Tis nice to meet ye, Doughall." She bit her lower lip, suddenly worried. "If I may call ye that."

"Of course. Laird MacLeod is the only one here with a title. Right, my friend?" Doughall clapped Broderick on the back and laughed as Broderick glared at him.

"Just ye wait, Doughall. Yer time will come and then ye can come back and tell me all aboot it."

"I fear that day has long passed. But I dinna mourn it. Nay, instead I'm free to roam as I choose."

Maggie was sure there was a history between the men, but she had no idea what. So instead of trying to understand, she watched the three men's interactions. As they all sat, and their mugs were filled with ale, and then refilled with more ale as the night wore on, she could tell that they were good friends that had known each other for a long time.

Doughall was funny and seemed carefree. Even with his dark hair and brown eyes, similar coloring to Diel, he didn't scare her. His personality was much too charming. And she didn't miss the looks he constantly received by both serving wenches and the maidens purposely walking past him.

A new jig started, and Broderick clapped his hands. "My favorite!" He exclaimed. "Maggie, fancy a dance?" His eyes twinkled and he gave her a wink as he held out his hand.

How could she say no to such an offer?

She placed her tiny hand in his and took delight in the sensation of his fingers wrapping around hers.

Broderick pulled her to her feet and they hurried past the tables the space where couples danced. Broderick's laugh was contagious as he lifted his knees and hopped from foot to foot to the beat of the music.

Maggie couldn't help but smile and join in. The last time she'd danced had been back in her village, but it wasn't with nearly as many people, but the memory of her mother and father laughing as they danced was forever emblazoned in her memory.

Broderick grabbed her hand and spun her around. She laughed and clapped her hands to the beat. They spun round and round and one song melded into another, and they kept dancing until Maggie couldn't catch her breath and was ready to collapse.

"Let's sit," Broderick laughed as he whisked her out of the crowd of dancers.

Mugs of ale were waiting for them when they took a seat and Maggie drank greedily, trying to quench her parched throat.

"Ye two seemed to be enjoying yourselves," Alastair quipped.

"Aye," Maggie agreed. "I havena danced so much since I was wee one. I forgot how much fun it can be."

"'Tis nice to see ye laugh, my lady."

She gave Alastair a genuine smile and nodded. It felt good to laugh. And Broderick had her laughing the whole time they were dancing. She was filled with pure joy and in this moment, she didn't have a care in the world. She had Broderick to thank for letting her escape the prison of her mind.

The place where her thoughts weren't very happy. The place where thoughts of revenge ran rampant.

And thoughts of leaving. She couldn't forget that Straik wasn't her home. She couldn't stay here.

Not if she was going to make Diel pay for what he'd done.

CHAPTER 12

The day started off beautifully. Maggie woke up in her bedchamber to the sun shining, taking the bite out of the air. She had plans to explore more of the lands today and spend time in the garden room. She was well aware after the weeks she'd spent at Straik that she was seeing it as home.

Her first mistake. Straik could never be her home. She had to avenge her family and friends.

She had to avenge herself and what Diel had stolen from her.

She sighed, blowing the breath loudly and most unlady-like out of her mouth. And Broderick.

He was her second mistake. She couldn't get the brawny warrior out of her mind. He occupied it day and night. The kind and caring way he spoke to her. Always genuine. He'd showered her with gifts. The soft wool cloak, slippers, her dress for the *cèilidh*. He'd even gifted her a beautiful dagger bedecked with a single jewel embedded in the hilt. It fit perfectly in her boot, and she never left her room without it.

The clansmen had taken a liking to him as well. She'd

heard the whispers about the castle and Una and Orna prattled on endlessly about how wonderful he is.

Even though Broderick didn't want to be laird, he'd been doing a fine job of showing that he had the skills to the lead the clan. He still hadn't found the killer of his brother and father, but Maggie knew he was working hard to do so.

Alastair, too. Maggie was glad that Broderick had such a fine mentor to lean on. He was one of a kind.

She threw off the furs and let out a squeal of surprise as the cool air pimpled her skin. The fire had gone out sometime during the night. Wrapping herself in a woolen shawl in MacLeod plaid, she poked at the embers, trying to bring them to life. A few sparked and she tossed in some kindling to get it going to a full fire again before adding a couple logs.

Stretching, her stomach growled. As if they had some kind of phenomenal bond, a knock sounded, bold and strong, and she instinctively knew it was Broderick.

Clutching the shawl tighter around herself, she opened the door to find him standing there, a tray full of probably one of everything Annag had available in the kitchens to break her fast. Something he'd done for the past sennight, and she looked forward to their morning chats. Sometimes they were quick conversations, but sometimes, if time permits, he would break his fast with her.

"Good morn," Broderick blessed Maggie with a brilliant smile. "Ye should break yer fast with hearty food if ye plan to go out and explore today."

Maggie laughed. "Is that food for me, or for ye? 'Tis way more than I could ever hope to consume."

"I've already broken my fast. Alastair and I are riding out shortly."

His lack of information didn't go unnoticed, but it wasn't her place to pry. But Orna had mentioned Straik was expecting a visitor, though she didn't say who. Mayhap

Doughall was returning. She enjoyed his company when he had visited previously.

She nodded. "I'm sure ye've a busy day ahead of ye."

"I do." He held up the tray. "May I?" He gestured toward the table.

"Of course. Pardon my manners." Maggie stepped aside and Broderick brushed by her as he deposited the tray on the table. "Are ye sure ye've eaten? There's more than enough food here to feed me, ye, and a healthy portion of the castle."

Broderick chuckled. "'Tis all for ye. An old," he paused as if carefully choosing the word to use. "Friend is arriving today."

So not Doughall then, she concluded.

"Alastair and I are going to meet to discuss the visit."

Maggie got the feeling he was purposely not telling her the whole story behind his guest, but even with as much as they've grown to know each other these past weeks, they were still strangers. And she had no business getting involved with castle affairs.

"Weel, I thank ye kindly for the generous meal. I will do my best to consume it all."

"Ye do no' need to do such a thing. 'Tis merely a variety of offerings so ye can choose what ye desire."

Desire.

The word bounced around in her mind often when Broderick was nearby. While she was in no place for a husband, when she was in Broderick's presence, she often desired for his touch. His nearness.

The desire conflicted with what Diel had done to her. Even though she knew Broderick would never treat her the way that monster had.

She knew not all men were like that beast. Her father, as an example, was a good man.

And Broderick. The man was very thoughtful and caring. Maggie enjoyed the special attention he gave her.

But that desire could also be a distraction. If she gave in to the pull of Broderick, it would only delay her revenge. Maggie couldn't let that happen. What if Diel was out there doing the same awful things to another innocent lass? She couldn't bear the thought.

Broderick cleared his throat. "I'll take my leave. Enjoy your walk. You're safe within the castle boundaries. If ye plan to venture to the woods, have a guard or two accompany ye. They'll ensure yer safety."

She couldn't help the smile that surfaced at his kindness and nodded her head. "I'll be sure to do so."

He paused, his intense blue eyes roaming over her. "Ye look especially bonny this morn, lass."

A giggle bubbled up from her chest. "I've only just woken up."

His gaze fell upon the bed and his eyes darkened to deep blue. "Aye."

"Oh," covering her mouth, her skin heated.

Taking a few steps forward, he stopped in front of her, so close she could feel the heat radiating off his body.

Her mouth was suddenly dry, and she licked her lips, trying to moisten them.

Broderick watched her mouth, his eyes hooded.

Time seemed to slow as he lowered his head to hers before he placed a kiss on her cheek, his full lips lingering on her skin.

Her breath hitched and she brought her hand up to her cheek when he stood and gave her a worried smile. "I'm sorry, lass."

"Dinna be," she whispered, her hand still lifted to her cheek.

He cleared his throat and cocked his head to the side. "I shall, er, take my leave. Enjoy yer walk, lass."

Maggie stood still, staring at the door Broderick closed quietly behind him.

He'd kissed her. On the cheek, but no less a kiss. And she quite liked it. She twirled in a circle, reliving the kiss in her mind, until a knock sounded, and she stopped abruptly, dizzy from the spinning.

Had Broderick returned? She tried to calm her breathing. "My lady?"

Maggie relaxed. It was Una. "Come in," she called.

Una's eyes rounded as she saw the vast amount of food Broderick had brought.

"I see Laird MacLeod visited ye again this morn."

"Och, aye. That he did."

Una raised a brow. "What has happened? Ye look like the cat who ate the wee mousy." She patted the bench instructing Maggie to sit and started running the comb through her hair.

Maggie was unsure whether she should divulge what had happened just before Una walked in the door. What if Broderick regretted his actions and it didn't happen again? Best to keep it their secret for now. But she was looking forward to their next meeting even more so than usual.

"'Tis nothing. Have ye broken yer fast?" Maggie asked studying the table and eyeing the delectable display laid out before them.

"I did, my lady."

"Una, please call me Maggie. I'm no' a lady."

Her maid smiled but didn't say she would. Instead, she moved around the room, straightening things up, making the bed, and pushed aside the draperies.

After she'd eaten, she dressed in her warmest clothes, including the cloak Broderick had gifted her and thought about her current circumstances.

If she wanted to leave the castle, she could. There was no one to stop her. Aye, Broderick told her to take guards with her if she was venturing into the woods, but they wouldn't know unless she told them.

She could wander there without a second glance from any of them and they wouldn't do anything to stop her. But she wasn't ready yet. To do so would require preparation on her part. She would need to pack a satchel and supplies and keep them away from prying eyes.

As much as she'd enjoyed her time here, it hadn't been helpful in helping her identify or locate Diel. The brooch was still her well-guarded secret. But it she believed it was time she brought it to Broderick's attention. Mayhap he would recognize the emblem.

In all the talks they've shared, Broderick approached her attack delicately. She understood that he wanted her to tell him everything. But if she did that, she knew he would track Diel down himself, and she didn't want him doing that. He'd said as much in their conversations.

But Diel was hers to kill.

She just needed more time.

OUTSIDE, the air was chilled by the cool breeze drifting in from the sea and Maggie drew the cloak in closer around her shoulders.

Inhaling deeply, she drew in the fresh, salty air and ignored the threat of rain that looked to be on the horizon.

With her stomach full from breaking her fast, she moved slowly, making her way around to the gardens. None of the flowers remained. They would bloom to life once again in the spring. But there was lots of green foliage to look at that thrived in the cold air.

She made her way to the ivy-covered archway and sat on the bench that had been placed there. Reaching deep into her pocket, she pulled out the brooch and unwrapped it from its fabric covering.

Studying it for the umpteenth time, Maggie wished there was a clan name engraved into the silver. It would make things so much easier. But like everything else, she had to work to learn Diel's identity.

Life hadn't been easy for her, she didn't expect the fates to suddenly change the path they'd laid out for her.

It was okay. She gladly accepted the challenge, and she wouldn't let it go until she'd found what she was looking for and put an end to his cruel ways.

Broderick had given her the dagger currently tucked snugly in her boot. When she saw him later tonight, she would ask him if he would be willing to train her in defense. She knew some basic moves. Enough so that Diel permanently held the mark of her fight on his face.

She rewrapped the brooch, winding the cloth back around the piece carefully and tucked it back into her pocket.

Broderick knew about it. Not exactly about the brooch, but he knew she was hiding something, but he'd been very gentlemanly about it and had not demanded she show him what she was hiding.

She made her way to the shore and looked out over the sea. The waves roiled to the surface, crested and broke, the sound had a calming effect and Maggie found a flat rock to sit on. She cradled her knees to her chest and watched the repeated motion.

The air was cooler near the water but she didn't mind, she just tucked her hands into the folds of the cloak to keep her fingers warm. She was in no rush to go back inside even though she knew she could sit in front of the fire and be warmed by the flames.

Thinking about everything that had transpired over the past month or so, she had so many people to thank for where she was now—healed from Diel's assault—and beyond happy that her courses had come, ensuring she didn't carry his babe in her belly. She'd never felt such relief when her aches started and the ensuing flow.

Maggie lost track of how long she'd been sitting there when she heard several horses stomping.

The mysterious visitor must be arriving.

Standing, she stretched and pondered returning to the castle. Not wanting to be in the way, she'd retire to her room so as not to disrupt whoever it was that was arriving.

Broderick hadn't mentioned anything about not being there to see his guest, but not being a true resident of Straik she didn't really have a place as far as being part of a welcoming party.

When Broderick spoke about the visit earlier, he gave the impression that it wasn't necessarily someone he thought highly of. The hesitation in his voice when he mentioned it earlier gave that away.

Walking up the path back to the castle, Maggie huddled into her shawl for warmth now that her time on the shore had allowed the cold to creep into her bones, she realized that the party had already arrived when she rounded the corner from the gardens.

Broderick and Alastair stood in the center of the courtyard waiting for their guest to dismount. Broderick's mouth was set into a firm line, and as she guessed earlier, he did not appear happy to see the person who's back was to her, but a foreboding feeling washed over her. She knew those movements.

That black hair.

Diel.

≈

MAGGIE'S HEART dropped to her gut, and she felt all the blood drain from her face. She tucked close to the wall, trying to flatten herself against it so she wouldn't be noticed.

What was Diel doing here? He'd found her. How?

She watched him dismount and stomp his boots into the ground. Those same boots that had stomped her body more than once.

Broderick stood cross-armed, his eyes, normally warm were the color of the icy depths of the sea. He didn't look pleased as Diel approached and clasped his shoulder in greeting. In fact, Broderick stiffened at the contact.

Unable to clearly hear their exchange, it was still easy to ready Broderick's body language. And he wasn't overly happy to see him.

Was Broderick going to send him away?

Maggie pulled the hood of her cloak over her head and covered her hair, trying to sink into obscurity.

Diel's coal-like gaze swept out over the courtyard, and she gasped as he looked in her direction. His eyes narrowed and the slightest sneer lifted the corner of his mouth.

She gasped and clamped a shaking hand over her mouth. Tears blurred her vision. Her heart raced, and the cold she'd felt earlier had been replaced with damp sweat. How was he here? The shock of seeing her tormentor had her frozen in place.

When the beast finally looked away, she let out the breath that had stuck in her throat. Swiping at the tears that flowed freely down her cheeks, she swallowed hard.

Instinct kicked in and no longer unable to move, she scurried into the castle. She ran up the stairs as fast she could. With the door closed, she threw the bolt and backed away as if Diel had followed her up the stairs and would come bursting forth any moment. She placed her hand on her heart, trying to slow her breathing.

Why wasn't Broderick demanding he leave? Did they know each other?

Was this their plan all along?

Nay. It couldn't be. Broderick had been much too kind to play a part in such a cruel scheme.

Diel was here. At Straik.

Escape was on Maggie's mind. She couldn't stay.

Diel was here, she repeated.

But wait, Maggie no longer had to hunt him down. It was as if fate had served him up on a silver platter. It was what she'd been dreaming of—finding Diel.

She frantically looked around the room. The room that Broderick had so painstakingly ensured it held all the comforts she needed. Her wardrobe was full of gowns and slippers. Each one ordered by him from the tailor. A pile of throws guaranteed she kept warm at night and the pillows allowed her to nestle into bed.

A room that was the exact opposite of the room Diel had kept her in. Maggie pushed that thought out of her mind.

There were no weapons in here, aside from the dagger in her boot. Unless she could somehow take him unawares, she would need more than that small knife. Even if she were to sneak into Broderick's chamber, any weapon in there would be much too heavy for her to wield.

The dilemma she found herself in was unnerving. What to do?

Stay and fight as was her plan since the time Diel had attacked her village? Or run and try to somehow track him down again when she was more prepared?

Her mind made up to leave, she studied the room. Her gaze falling on the items Broderick had kindly given her.

Though she wanted to take everything, she needed to be practical.

Being loaded down with an armful of belongings would only slow her down. The boots she wore would offer her feet protection against the sharp rocks and branches, unlike the last time she'd been running through the woods. She laid out a plaid and added her clothing, not a lot, another dress, a chemise, the pair of slippers Broderick had so proudly ordered made for her, and a shawl. From the table she grabbed some food that she could easily tuck away and eat later.

Maggie's hands shook uncontrollably, spilling the ale she was trying to pour all over the table. She was trying to settle her nerves. But her hands remained unsteady, and she gave up on the ale. The pitcher clattered to the table, and she snapped her gaze to the door, expecting it to burst open in any moment. She swiped at the tears running down her cheeks.

Her goal had been to find Diel. His unexpected appearance was shocking. And terrifying. Why was he here?

Was she the reason?

And what role did Broderick play in all this? Her mind was jumping from one thought to the next, making her stomach turn.

Did Diel know she'd been here all along? She'd been here for weeks without a sign from the brute. Surely, he hadn't been watching her all this time, had he? The thought was distressing. To think when she had been wandering the grounds he could have been out there watching her every move.

Fighting the urge to fall to the floor and weep, she moved to the window and looked out over the courtyard. The traveling party was still there. Broderick, Diel, and Alastair were speaking tensely, all three men stood stiff and on edge.

Maggie survived Diel once before and she would again. Sitting on the bed, she pushed her bundle of goods away from her.

It was her time to fight. Deep in her heart, she knew she could trust Broderick, though that little voice was on her shoulder telling her she shouldn't. His actions spoke louder than words and those actions had been naught but caring and kind.

With her mind made up, she took a deep breath and pulled the dagger from her boot, the sharp blade glistening in the light. She would have to move smartly and quickly.

And when Diel was least expecting it.

CHAPTER 13

*B*roderick waited for his childhood nemesis to dismount from his horse and fought to keep the scowl off his face.

Alastair stood stoically by his side, arms crossed, feet planted to the ground. He leaned toward Broderick. "Ye are in yer rightful place."

Broderick knew it was supposed to be an affirmation, but he couldn't help that feeling of hurt when he was younger, and his father chose Duff over him.

It was a daft thought. He viewed Alastair as his father. The man was everything to him and loved him like the son he'd lost.

Duff MacDonald approached Broderick with a sneer on his face. "Brod...pardon, Laird MacLeod." He clasped Broderick's shoulder and Broderick held back from punching him square in the jaw.

"Duff. I'm surprised ye came back."

Duff raised his black brows. "Why would I no'? Straik has been my home for years."

"Ye didna come to pay yer respects to my da and brother.

I was a bit surprised since ye'd been raised as if ye were Callum's son."

"'Twas my plan, but alas, I wasna able to."

They stood, staring each other down.

"Are ye going to invite me in? 'Twas a long journey. My men and I could use a drink."

Broderick bit his tongue. He wanted to wipe that smug grin off his face and grind it into the dirt. Instead, he smiled and decided to be the bigger man. "Of course. Ye and yer men are welcome inside for a drink and a meal."

Inside the Great Hall, Duff's men were just as Broderick thought they would be—loud, boisterous, and rude to the help.

Duff and Broderick sat at a table near the center of the hall, a pitcher of ale between them.

"The clan seems to be thriving. I'm surprised *ye* came back." Duff slurped his ale and wiped his mouth with his arm.

"My father and brother were murdered. The lairdship fell on me. The choice was no' mine." Broderick kept his voice even. He didn't want any of the clansmen to think he didn't want to be here. But most of all he didn't want to give Duff any indication that he'd had doubts about returning.

"Callum wouldna have expected such a turn of events." Duff belched loudly and tapped his chest.

Broderick shot him a look of disgust and took a long sip of ale, studying Duff over the rim of his cup. The man had no manners whatsoever. "What do ye think he would have expected? Someone needed to take on the clan responsibility."

Duff dipped his head. "Aye. Though I didna think it would be ye."

Broderick sighed, tired of the game Duff was playing. "Ye thought it would be ye?" He pierced his childhood enemy with a look that had made lesser men shrink in fear. "Ye want to lead a clan, go back to yer own. The MacLeod is mine."

Duff barked out a laugh and clapped Broderick on the back. "Ye jest my old friend."

Broderick didn't return the laughter. He was dead serious. Duff could go back to the MacDonald. He had no claim to the MacLeod clan.

Duff pointed his finger at Broderick. "Ye've grown into yerself in the years ye've been away." A serving wench passed, and Duff reached out and grabbed her behind. The lass shrunk back from his touch.

"Dinna touch the help. They're not here for yer pleasure."

"Weel, aren't ye the honorable one? The wenches are used to it. They ken me."

"'Tis not yer clan. 'Tis mine. And the serving lasses can roam about their duties free of worry that they are going to be harassed by ye or yer men. Put the word out. All of them are to be treated with respect. If I catch one of yer men mistreating any of my castlefolk, they'll have me to deal with. And they will no longer be allowed within Straik's walls."

"Och, ye've really taken on the role of laird, Broderick. I'm impressed."

Broderick didn't need Duff's fake accolades. He pushed back from the table, the chair screeching on the stone floor. "I've got duties to attend to. Ye are welcome to sup and drink to yer fill. The maids will show ye to yer quarters."

"Aye." Duff held up his mug in a sarcastic cheer. "I shall. Is it a wife ye're running to?"

Broderick thought of Maggie. He hadn't seen her since this morning when he'd brought her the tray of food to break her fast.

He had no interest in telling Duff about Maggie. In fact, he planned to keep him as far away from her as he could. But servants talk. Duff would find out about her soon enough.

"I've no wife, but other pressing matters." A scene of Maggie as his wife ran through his mind. He could picture her as his betrothed. His kiss earlier this morn surprised him as much as it had Maggie. He'd dreamt of kissing her. But he didn't want to be too forward. She needed to move at her own pace. For this, he could be a patient man. But no matter how much time passed, he saw a future between them.

Hopefully, Maggie did, too. He planned to spend the rest of his life showing her she deserved to be loved. No one deserved to go through the ordeal she had been through. When she was ready, he'd be waiting.

"I dinna ken how ye plan to remain laird with no wife." Duff threw out the statement as he was walking away.

Broderick should have ignored it. He knew Duff was just trying to bait him. And he fell right into the trap.

He spun on his heel and rounded on Duff. "My father managed for years. I'm sure I can do the same."

Duff scoffed. "Yer father already had an heir. He didna need a new wife." He sipped his ale and wiped his mouth with the back of his hand again before slamming his mug on the table. "'Tis no' the same situation."

Broderick left the Great Hall without responding. He wanted to see Maggie. The pull he felt every moment of the day to see her was hard to deny. Everything he saw throughout the day reminded him of Maggie.

The musical notes of a bird reminded him of Maggie's lyrical voice.

The sun in the sky reminded him of the light in her eyes.

The sparks in a flame reminded him of her fiery spirit.

He threw his head back and groaned. He was falling. And he knew it.

Taking the steps two at a time, he made his way up to the second floor that housed the sleeping chambers, but most importantly, Maggie's bedchamber.

Broderick knocked softly and then waited.

And waited.

He frowned when Maggie didn't answer the door.

He rapped his knuckles against the wood again. "Maggie?" He listened but couldn't hear any movement on the inside. He knocked again, with a little more force. He was starting to worry. "Maggie, lass. Is everything alright?"

CHAPTER 14

*M*aggie listened to Broderick's knocks and then his pleas, but she was frozen in fear. There was every possibility that Diel was with him. She'd seen them enter the castle together.

How could she have been so stupid? While she'd been here letting her guard down and letting Broderick in, was he plotting along with Diel this whole time? Betrayal hung heavy in the air around her, weighing her down, stealing her breath.

"Maggie? Ye have me worried. Open the door."

She heard the pleading in his voice, and it shot straight to her heart. She didn't want Broderick worrying about her. But she also needed to think of herself and her safety.

Conflicted. That's what her feelings were. Warring against each other within her soul. One second, she was reminded of Broderick's thoughtfulness and his caring ways, and the next she was wondering if he was going to bring her to Diel.

She approached the door but didn't unlatch it. "Are ye alone?"

"Pardon?" He sounded taken aback by her question.

"Are ye alone?" she asked again, her voice a little louder than before.

"Of course, I am. Why would I no' be?"

A wee bit of relief washed over her, relaxing her shoulders, but only a little. Broderick had always been nothing but honest in their conversations. Hadn't he? Why would he start lying now?

Inhaling a deep breath, she grasped the latch, slowly lifting it to unlock the door.

Broderick stood there, his brows furrowed, but he didn't look angry. He looked concerned.

"Ye latched yer door?"

Her feet were frozen in place. She wanted to look out into the hall. To ensure no one else was there, but she couldn't move.

"Lass," he approached her slowly. "What is it? Ye look as if ye've seen a ghost."

She made her way around him and slammed the door shut and dropped the latch into place once more. Realizing that it meant that she was now locked in her room alone with Broderick. But surprisingly, that's not what worried her.

Maggie twirled around and stared at Broderick.

She couldn't slow her racing heart. Putting a hand on her chest, she willed her breathing to slow, but panic mixed with anger rose to a high level. With this reaction how did she ever expect to take Diel down? She saw him from afar and she was acting like he was in the same room with her.

Mayhap he was. Mayhap the person she'd trusted the most was her true enemy. Mayhap she was locked in her room with a man that was going to hand her over to the monster that had nearly killed her.

Was he only pulling the wool over her eyes to make her

comfortable? Was it to ensure she didn't run while he waited for Diel to arrive?

Why would he do such a thing?

Broderick glanced around the room and his eyes set on the open plaid with her items thrown hastily in the center and his forehead creased.

"Are ye going somewhere?" Concern laced his voice. He glanced at the door, back to the bed, and then his eyes settled on her. "Lass, I dinna ken what is happening. I just ken that something is amiss. Talk to me."

Oh, she wanted to. She really did. She wanted to tell him everything. But was he trustworthy? Or was he her enemy, too? Confusion clouded her mind.

She'd told no one about everything she'd suffered through at the hands of Diel.

She needed Broderick's help to take Diel down.

Even though she wanted to do that herself, doubt crept in on her capability of actually being able to do it.

But she needed his help. His plagued expression seemed genuine. And looking back to the way he'd greeted Diel, she wasn't entirely sure that Broderick welcomed his visit.

Maggie sighed and walked to the bedside table, opened the drawer, and pulled out the linen wrapped brooch.

She handed it to Broderick.

"What's this?"

"Open it."

He turned the package over in his hands. "Are ye sure?"

"Aye. Please."

Slowly, he unfurled the fabric and uncovered the brooch. His eyes widened with recognition when he saw what it was.

He frowned, and his eyes narrowed as he studied her face. "Why do ye have Duff's brooch?"

"Duff?" Was that Diel's real name?

"Aye. 'Tis a MacDonald brooch, but only Duff and his men have this style."

Maggie couldn't stop the tears that dropped from her eyes, and she sniffed, swiping at her nose.

"That brooch was dropped," she paused, a sob bursting violently from her throat. "When I was left for dead...in the woods...by the men who left me there." Sobbing uncontrollably, Maggie couldn't stop shaking. She'd finally put a voice to her past.

Broderick's guttural roar was unlike anything she'd ever heard before. But she didn't shrink back in fear. She knew it wasn't meant for her.

He closed the brooch in his fist, his knuckles white. "Duff. Duff is the one who hurt ye?" He nodded his head, clenching his jaw. "Of course he was. The vile bastard."

"I dinna ken his name. He never spoke it in the time I'd been held. I called him Diel." She sniffed and swiped at her cheeks. "When I returned from my walk, I saw him in the courtyard. His face is one I canna forget."

BRODERICK'S BLOOD BOILED. Duff was the one who'd ravaged Maggie.

And now he was here

With Maggie.

No wonder she'd latched the door.

"Maggie." He let her name hang in the air. What could he say? What must she be thinking?

Spinning on him she pierced him with a glare fierce as fire. "Is he one of yer men?" she asked, accusation lacing her voice.

"Nay. Absolutely no'."

"Then why is he here? How did he find me?"

Broderick felt the emotion roiling off Maggie. Anger darkened her eyes to the color of the darkest night sky.

"Ye know him." She threw up her hands and began to pace around the room. "I've been such a fool. A fool! 'Twas all a ruse. I should have known."

"Maggie, lass."

"Och, nay. Dinna 'Maggie, lass' me," she spat, shaking her head sharply.

"'Tis no' what ye think. He grew up here."

"That bastard took everything from me. Everything," she repeated. "He killed my family, my friends, and och, weel, ye ken verra well what else he did to me."

The room suddenly seemed small. Too small to hold in the anger they both felt. He well understood Maggie's reaction. Straik was a place she'd finally become comfortable in. She'd taken a liking to the clansfolk here and they did the same with her. But now, the world she'd known has been turned on its heel. What else was the brute capable of? A niggling feeling started to throb at the base of his skull.

Callum and Ewan.

Was it possible that Duff was behind their killings? That the ambush was set up to get rid of the first and second in line so that Duff could become laird?

It was a probability, and one that he would ponder later when he could speak with Alastair. But right now, he had to give his full attention to Maggie. Her safety was first and foremost on his mind. Everything she'd gone through at the hands of Duff. Visions of her ordeal filled his mind. The urge to run out to the Great Hall and rip Duff's limbs from his body one by one was so strong.

But he couldn't leave Maggie. Not in this state. And not with her believing that he played a part in this evil that she'd been subject to.

Walking to the side table, Maggie sloppily poured a

mugful of ale and drank it quickly. She blew out a breath as she refilled the mug before turning to him once more, cup in hand, her eyes searching his face.

What was she looking for? The truth? Broderick hoped she could see the sincerity in his gaze when their eyes met. "I would ne'er do anything to hurt ye, lass. Duff's presence here is an unwelcome one."

Finally, she must have believed his words. Her shoulders dropped just slightly, not in defeat, but in acknowledgement.

Taking a step forward Broderick opened his arms and waited to see if Maggie would accept his embrace. He just wanted to hold her in his arms. To show her that he was being truthful. To show her that he could be trusted.

Maggie set the cup down on the table and stood there, her eyes darting from his face to his arms for what seemed like hours, but was only moments, and finally stepped forward. He enveloped her in his warmth and closed his eyes in relief. Thankful that she wasn't frightened of him. He inhaled her sweet scent and if circumstances were different, he would have taken the time to savor the moment. "He doesna ken ye are here."

"He may. When I walked back from the shore and I had first seen him…" she took a deep, shaky breath. "I was frozen in place, and I felt like he smiled at me. A most sinister smile."

"Shite," Broderick cursed. "I dinna mention yer name to him, lass, nor is he aware of yer presence here from what I understand."

"Then why is he here?" She buried her face into his chest, and it took all his strength not to squeeze her tighter.

"Remember when I told ye of the lad my father fostered when I was young? The one that he treated as his second son instead of me?"

She nodded against him but didn't speak.

"That lad was Duff. We've been enemies since as long as I can remember. And right now, I want to slit his throat."

Maggie pushed off his chest, breaking their embrace and walked to the window. "Ever since I arrived at Straik, I've been plotting my revenge. His death. I've had dreams of how I would land the death blow." She kept her back to Broderick, staring out over the grounds below. "That brooch was the only clue I had to his identity."

"I ken why ye didna tell me. But I hope ye ken ye can trust me wholeheartedly, Maggie."

"I do."

The pain in her voice was like a knife straight to his heart. The compulsion to go downstairs and find the bastard that had caused Maggie so much pain and rip him apart burned Broderick's insides. But as much as he wanted to take the lead, he knew he couldn't.

Nay, this was Maggie's fight. And he would support her fully.

"What do ye want to do?"

She spun and looked at him square in the eye. "I want him dead. I want it so he can never hurt another woman again."

"Aye," he agreed, understanding the direction of her thoughts as they matched his own. "Ye've been a fighter e'er since that day I found ye in the woods. Even then I knew ye were a warrior. One that I would be proud to have by my side."

BRODERICK'S KIND words lit a fire in Maggie's belly. A fire that she welcomed and didn't want to tamp down. She was terrified that Diel, no, Duff, was just two floors below her. His actual name fit him. It still sounded evil. His parents had chosen the right moniker for such a dark soul.

Gazing at Broderick his body stance told her that he was on her side. His hands fisted at his side, he was fit to be tied. Anger rolled over him in waves. She could feel it, but it didn't frighten her. She knew it was aimed at Duff. It was nice to have someone support her with all his being. Something she was thankful for. Maggie needed his support right now.

"My mind is all addled. He's stolen my thoughts for so long, that I dinna ken what to do. I dinna want to leave this room."

"I made a vow to ye before that ye are safe here. Always." He brushed his hands through his blond hair and locked eyes with her. "I will do everything in my power to make sure no harm comes to ye."

His voice was sincere, but strong. Until the night her village was attached, she'd never thought about being in this type of situation. She'd always thought her parents would be by her side. That she would watch them grow old together. When Duff attack and rained his evil down on them, Maggie didn't know how she would survive. Then Duff attacked her and once again she didn't know how she would survive, only that she needed to.

How she would have loved to have Broderick as a protector then. Mayhap none of this would have happened. But she couldn't live in a world of what ifs. What had been done was done and she couldn't change the past.

But she could control her future. And Broderick was here to support her every step of the way. Maggie believed him when he said he wouldn't let anyone hurt her.

But she still needed to deal with Duff.

"I need to speak with Alastair." Broderick broke the silence and jarred Maggie from her thoughts.

Her heart jumped. He was going to leave her alone. Blood pounded in her veins, and she started to sweat. What if Duff came and barreled through the door while Broderick was gone? "I dinna want to be alone." As much as she wanted to make Duff pay for her sins, she wasn't sure she was ready to be alone yet.

Broderick approached, taking her hands in his. "Lass, I canna have that bastard walking my halls. I need to get to Alastair and have he and my men detain him. 'Tis been a long time since Straik's dungeons have been put to use. This is the perfect reason until we, ye, decide what needs to be done with the louse."

Maggie wanted to simultaneously burst into tears and grab the nearest weapon, her dagger.

He brought her hand up to his lips and placed a kiss on the sensitive skin there. His warm hand pulled her into an embrace, and she just wanted to stay snuggled into the safety of his chest for eternity.

"We're going to free ye from yer demons. I promise. I willna be gone long but latch the door behind me. I'll send up yer maid to stay with ye so ye have someone to pass the time with. Open the door for only her and I. Understand?"

She bobbed her head in agreement.

"I willna be gone long."

"Be careful," she whispered. Broderick was a strong warrior, and she had no doubt in his skills against Duff. But she also knew that Duff wouldn't fight fair.

"Dinna fash, lass." He dipped and brought his mouth to hers, capturing her lips in a passionate kiss that claimed her as his.

Not wanting the kiss to end, she brought her arms up and wrapped them around his neck, wishing everything else would just fall away and that they could stay like this forever.

"I must go," he murmured against her lips. "But dinna fash, we can continue this later."

Maggie smiled at Broderick's attempt to lighten the

mood. Her hand went to her swollen lips—swollen from passion—not pain.

Such a gentle gesture from such a strong man and she didn't miss the difference between that and the cruelty of Duff.

Cruelty that she refused to let rule her life any longer.

"Remember, latch the door. I will stay until I hear it fall into place."

"I will." She had no intention of just staying in the open like prey.

Maggie waited until he closed the door behind him and then brought down the latch.

Broderick knocked. "I'll be back soon."

She placed her palm on the door. The events of the day had been almost too much for her to take. She prayed Broderick would stay safe and remain vigilant. Duff was not to be trusted in any way.

A soft knock sounded, and she backed away from the door. Fear instantly taking hold until she heard Una's voice. "My lady, Laird MacLeod sent me."

Maggie breathed a sigh of relief and lifted the latch. Opening the door, she grabbed Una's hand and pulled her inside before quickly bringing the latch down once again securing them in the room.

CHAPTER 15

"*A*lastair." Broderick found his mentor near the kitchens speaking to one of the kitchen maids. "I need to talk to ye. 'Tis urgent."

Concern crossed Alastair's weathered features, but he didn't question Broderick. Just followed him down the hall and then up the stairs to Broderick's bedchamber.

With the door shut behind them Broderick addressed his mentor. "Do ye ken where Duff is?"

Alastair raised a brow and shrugged. "I last saw him in the Great Hall. He was having his share of ale. I had to tell him to keep his hands to himself."

Broderick shook his head. "I'd had the same conversation with him. I need ye and a few men to find him and secure him in the dungeon."

"What?" Alastair raised his eyebrows in surprise.

"Aye. I'd do it myself, but I'm afraid the second I lay my eyes on him, I'll detach his head from his body."

"What's happened?"

"'Tis Maggie."

"Is the lass unwell?"

"Nay. Aye." Broderick pushed his hands through his hair. "That bastard. He's the vile beast that attacked her."

"How do ye ken?" Alastair leaned a hip on the large sideboard set against the wall.

"Maggie. She saw him when he arrived, and she was walking back from walking the shore. Everything that was done to her. Including leaving her in the woods to die, was done by Duff." Broderick turned to the wall and slammed his palm against the stone. He wanted to punch it but couldn't afford to break the bones in his hand, but he'd gladly break them while beating Duff's skull in.

"That fecking bastard. I ken he was brutal, but no' to that extent."

"He'll be dealt with. How is up to Maggie. She endured his cruelty. 'Tis the only way." Broderick paced the room, hands fisted at his sides.

"Aye. But will she be able to?"

"I've no doubt. She's been planning her revenge her whole time here."

Alastair smiled at that information. "She's a spitfire that one."

Pride welled up in Broderick's chest. Maggie was. Just as he'd thought when he'd first met her, the lass had a warrior's soul.

Pushing off the desk, Alastair ambled to the door, his slight limp the only indication that the man's body wasn't at its peak. "I'll get him to the dungeon. What of his men?"

Broderick looked toward the window. As much as he wanted to banish them all from Straik, he couldn't do that. Not yet. "Line them up for questioning. I want to know who was involved."

"Aye." Alastair paused with his hand on the door handle. "What are ye going to do?"

"I'm going to stay the night with Maggie. She's strong but

she's terrified. Her maid is with her now, but she willna be able to protect her."

"I'll be sure he is imprisoned, my laird." Alastair pounded his fist to his chest and turned on his heel. Outside the room Broderick heard him call to a few men.

He had no doubt they would get Duff to the dungeons. Broderick wanted to do it himself, but he worried about Maggie. Her well-being was his main concern.

It was his duty to keep her safe. He'd promised her he would. And today, he felt like he'd broken that promise by welcoming her attacker into his castle. The castle that he hoped one day she would see as her home.

He couldn't deny the feelings that were growing between them. Their last kiss had affected him more than he let her know. Broderick was sure the last thing on Maggie's mind was a man—or a husband, though she had warmed to him, and he thought she might be feeling that same spark. After everything she'd endured, it was understandable that she was in no rush to move forward with something she'd only associated with pain and terror.

Broderick cursed as he thought of all the ways he wanted to hurt Duff.

Now that Duff had been caught and they could deal with him, Maggie no longer had to feel in danger.

Rushing back up the stairs, he knocked on Maggie's door, announcing himself so she knew to open the door.

Wood scratched against wood as the latch was lifted and the door opened. Una stood aside, allowing him to enter the room. Maggie was sitting in the chair by the fire, her back stiff, but she looked relieved to see him.

"My lady, do ye need me to stay?"

Broderick remained silent. The question was a formality, he knew. Everyone had seen he and Maggie interact and spend time together, both alone and with others.

"Nay. Ye may go, Una. Thank ye for staying with me until Laird MacLeod returned."

Una dipped into a curtsy and left the room.

"It seems ye two get on well."

"Aye. She's very sweet and attentive. And she's also great to talk to when I need someone to listen."

"Ye can talk to me. I'll gladly listen to whatever ye might have to say."

Her pink lips lifted in the corners. Almost a smile, but his attempt at a jest was misplaced and he wanted to kick himself for being such a fool.

"Alastair is moving Duff to the dungeons as we speak. I think it will be good for him to languish there for the night wondering why. Tonight, we can discuss yer strategy."

MAGGIE'S STRATEGY. She was touched that Broderick was treating her as one of his warriors. If she was still living in her croft, the idea of a warrior laird talking to her as if she were one of them would have never crossed her mind. It didn't seem plausible.

What was her strategy? Duff was imprisoned. As much as she wanted to, she couldn't go to the cell and strike him down.

Though in her mind's eye, that's all that she saw. Her hand raised, knife clenched in her fist as she brought it down and sank it deep into Duff's chest.

She wasn't a killer, but she'd never wanted something so bad in all her life.

"Are ye sure he's secured?" The possibility of him escaping his cell and finding her had her wanting to wither into the dark corners so that he might not find her.

"Aye. With men standing guard."

"What have ye told him?"

"He knows naught. I've ordered Alastair no' to mention a word and definitely no' to mention yer name. If ye want to face him tomorrow, ye'll have yer chance and he won't know ye're coming."

She sighed, her body shaking from her nerves being on edge.

She didn't know how she would face him. The thought of being in close proximity with him again left her terrified.

"Ye dinna need to do anything ye dinna want."

Broderick was so observant to pick up on her thoughts. Her bedchamber seemed small with him in it. His presence took up so much of the space. But she rather liked him being here.

She enjoyed his closeness. Even with Duff locked away in the dungeons deep in the belly of the castle, when Maggie should be concocting plans of his demise, she could only think of Broderick.

His touch. His kisses.

She wanted more of them. She sighed. Mayhap in the future when Duff had paid for his sins, she and Broderick could concentrate on more pleasant things.

For now, with Broderick here, she felt protected. There was no way Duff would get to her. But it didn't stop the gooseflesh from standing up on her arms, or her breath to catch whenever she heard noises outside her door.

There was that part of her mind that didn't want to believe that they would be able to keep Duff locked away all night. He was conniving and manipulative. What if he talked his way out of his cell? Would he go room to room trying to find her? Set the place ablaze? She didn't want to be the reason Straik was burnt to the ground.

"What are ye thinking, lass?"

She gazed at Broderick and for the first time, she noticed

that he had his sword strapped to his side. The huge broadsword was nearly as tall as he was and looked menacing, but beautiful. The handle was decorated with jewels embedded into the intricate design carved into the steel.

A worthy sword for a worthy warrior.

It matched the dagger he'd given her. Warmth spread through her at the knowledge that he'd gifted her something so important to him.

"I have so many thoughts running amok in my mind. How I've been waiting for this day since the day he killed my family. All this time, I've pictured this very scenario. So many times. But I never thought it would happen here with him arriving at his own volition."

Broderick poured a mug of ale and handed it to her. "Drink, lass. It will settle yer nerves."

She accepted the cup and drank. More deeply than she normally would and savored the burn that settled in her chest.

"I'm terrified he's going to somehow manipulate his way out of his prison and I'm going to look up and he's going to be right there, looming over me.

"I promise ye, he willna."

She nodded and looked toward the door. The wood was thicker and stronger than the door leading into her croft had been. And this door wasn't the first band of resistance. And she had the added protection from the sturdy latch, nestled snuggly in its black iron brackets.

She laughed at the thought that she felt much safer in her croft with minimal protection than she did here with all the protection in the world. But then she had never thought her village would have been attacked, razed, and her fellow villagers murdered.

"I believe ye are speaking the truth. Pardon that I have some reservations."

He dipped his head in acquiescence. "I'll be here to protect ye. I know I keep repeating myself, but 'tis true. I want ye to feel safe."

"I do." With Broderick near, she wasn't fearful. But he couldn't stay here. Not because she didn't want him to. Maggie certainly wanted nothing more because she loved having him close.

But she needed to be the one to confront Diel. And she wanted to do so alone. If he didn't know she was here, she had the element of surprise. At this point she wasn't entirely sure if Duff had really seen her earlier or if it was her mind playing tricks. He may still think she died in the woods. She needed a plan to get around the guards that Broderick said he'd had posted outside of the cell.

"I do feel safe. That's because of ye."

Broderick beamed and placed a kiss on her forehead before settling into the other chair near the fire.

"What are ye plans for the evening?" Maggie asked, curious to hear if he really planned to spend the night in her room, because that's what she believed he was thinking.

"I'll be here, ensuring your safety."

Biting her lower lip, she studied his features. His strong, chiseled jaw was set. His blue eyes determined. The model warrior and laird. But surely, he was eager to get his own hands on Duff.

She took a deep breath, trying to gain the courage to tell him that she didn't want him to spend the night with her. "I appreciate yer kindness, Broderick. But—."

His head snapped to hers, his forehead creased. "But what?"

What reason could she give for him not to take offense that she wanted to be alone tonight? "'Tis no' proper for ye to be alone with me all night long. Think of what the castle folk will say when they find out in the morning."

He rubbed his chin, the stubble making a scratchy sound that seemed to echo off the chamber's walls from the otherwise silence in the room. "I canna protect ye if I'm no' here."

"Nonsense. Ye have men watching him in the dungeons, ensuring that he doesna escape."

"Aye, but ye said earlier that ye still feared that he may somehow get out."

She sighed. "My nerves rule my tongue sometimes. I dinna truly believe that. I know ye are doing everything in yer power to see to it that Diel stays put. I trust in ye."

Those words seemed to do the trick. Maggie watched as Broderick's shoulders relaxed a bit as the tension that had kept them coiled released from his body.

"I'll keep the door barricaded and willna open it for anyone other than ye or Una." A tinge of guilt pulled at her gut. She didn't want to lie to Broderick, but she had no intention of letting Una in.

Maggie could tell he was conflicted, but he finally acquiesced.

"Do ye still have the dagger I gave ye?"

She reached into her boot and pulled out the dagger, showing him she still had it. She didn't tell him that she went nowhere without it.

Broderick grinned. "Good. Remember how I showed ye to use it? To strike with force?"

"Aye," Maggie nodded.

"If anyone comes near ye or threatens ye in any way, dinna hesitate to use it."

"I willna need to as no one is getting through that door."

The dagger was what she would use to put an end to Diel's terror.

CHAPTER 16

*O*ut in the courtyard a short while later, Broderick studied the men that Alastair had lined up against the wall.

Duff's men.

They all held the same sneer that was always so prevalent on Duff's face. A prerequisite of being one of his fighters it seemed.

"I'm Laird MacLeod," he announced, his voice strong and steady, even though it seemed odd to his ears.

A few of the men snickered and Broderick pierced them each with a glare.

"Have ye something to say about that?"

One of the men matched his stare and spoke up. "Aye. Ye've nay right to claim the lairdship. No' after abandoning the MacLeod all those years ago."

Broderick clasped his hands behind his back. "I did leave Straik a long time ago. Had vowed to ne'er step foot in it again. But things change. The deaths of my father and brother changed the trajectory of where I thought my life was leading."

"'Tis a power grab by Alastair. He kens damn well Duff should be laird."

Alastair stood stoically, his arms crossed, mouth in a thin line, but said nothing. He was letting Broderick take the lead on this one. As he should, but it still felt odd to Broderick.

"Duff isna a MacLeod. If he wants to be laird, he can return to the MacDonald." He knew Duff wouldn't be leaving MacLeod lands with a breath left in his body.

"Ye turned yer back on the MacLeod." Another of Duff's men declared.

"Aye. With the assumption Ewan would be laird when my father passed. Them being brutally cut down together was ne'er foreseen." Broderick pierced each of the men with a look to show them he had his suspicions. "So here I am. Called back to take my place as laird. But enough of the semantics. Where have you and Duff been in these past few months?"

"Why should we tell ye?"

Broderick closed the distance and grabbed the man by his tunic. "Because," he stated through gritted teeth. "As we've established, *I'm* the laird now."

The sod snarled, his rotted teeth on full display. "Looks like ye've grown up from the useless welp ye used to be as a lad."

Broderick flattened his hand to his chest and pushed against the wall.

"Who wants to tell me where Duff was before coming here?" He eyed the men before him. A few of them stood still, glaring at Broderick and not saying a word. One or two shuffled from one foot to the other. He figured they were probably his best bet to finding out Duff's whereabouts.

"Anybody going to talk?" Broderick asked, scanning the men's faces.

They remained silent.

"Alastair?" Broderick walked away from the men and cocked his head to the side, motioning for him to follow. "I dinna think we are going to make any headway with them together as a group. I think it best we separate them and talk to them one at a time."

"That makes sense." Alastair nodded. "If they aren't near each other, they're no longer a united front and they won't ken what the other is saying and who might be loose-lipped."

"Aye. Gather a few men and let's get these bastards in separate places."

Dipping his head in acknowledgement, Alastair moved toward the men, and yanked a man from the line.

The man who spoke earlier spat on the ground at Broderick's feet. "Ye canna just hold us here."

"I can and I will. Mayhap if ye give me the information I'm seeking, ye'll gain yer freedom. Mayhap."

"Duff will have yer head for this," he said.

Broderick barked out a laugh. "Pray tell, how?"

"Ye will see. Ye underestimate him."

Broderick walked away, tired of the empty threats. Right now, his only concern was Maggie and keeping her safe. He was a wee bit sad that she didn't want him staying the night with her to make sure no one got into her room. But he also understood her hesitation.

He'd known Duff was a bastard since they were young, but even Broderick didn't think he would ever do such a horrendous thing. Where the hell had he been before he arrived here? Had his father sent him on a mission?

Or was the sneaking suspicion he had that Duff had something to do with his father and brother's demise true?

～

After separating Duff's men and assigning guards to each of them, Broderick and Alastair dragged one of them to a room deep in the castle near the dungeon cells, but far enough away that Duff would be unable to hear what was going on.

The bastard dug his heels in and kept trying to jerk away.

"If ye dinna stop fighting and start walking, I will make sure ye canna fight and carry ye down peacefully." Broderick was getting tired of his resistance.

He studied Broderick for a brief second before standing and walking on his own accord.

"See, was that so hard?" Alastair led him to a room that held a small table in one corner and a chair on the opposite side and promptly shoved him onto it.

Alastair shut the door and Broderick leaned against the cool stone wall. The room was dark. A single candle flickering added the only light.

"Now, tell me where ye were before arriving at Straik." Broderick studied his nails as he waited for a reply. He didn't want the man to think he was eagerly waiting for his answer, though he wanted to wrap his hands around the bastard's throat and throttle him until he gave him the information he needed.

The man remained silent.

"Listen," Broderick stated. "Ye can tell me now, when no-one else can hear ye or ye can rot."

Still, not a word was spoken.

Alastair approached and landed a solid punch to the man's jaw. His head snapped to the side and blood flew from his mouth.

Broderick raised a brow at his mentor. It had been a long time since they'd been in combat together. Most days Alastair delegated the missions for the Amadán, but rarely fought himself. He must be missing those days.

Alastair shrugged and gave Broderick a smirk.

"Ye bastard!" The cretin turned his head and spit blood.

"What's yer name?" Broderick tried a different tactic. Mayhap he needed to start small. They were Duff's men after all.

"I'm no' telling ye shite. Ye can find someone else 'cause it willna be me."

Broderick looked at Alastair, "Do ye recognize him?" Since he'd been here when Duff was.

"Nay. I havena seen him afore." Alastair swatted the man in the back of the head.

He glared at Broderick and Alastair but remained silent.

"Fine. Alastair, detain him in one of the cells." Broderick added, "Away from Duff."

"Aye, my laird."

"And bring the next one down. Ye can get his guard to help ye haul him if he doesna cooperate."

Alastair grabbed the man's neck and led him out the door. The man continued to threaten about how Duff would have their heads for this.

Broderick was frustrated and anger welled inside him. As time passed, it became harder to contain. Having Duff locked in a dank cell was a small consolation. The bastard needed to be dead. But that was Maggie's deed to carry out. If she wished.

If the time came and she couldn't go through with it, he would gladly sink his blade into the retch's black heart. Because one thing was for certain—Duff was not leaving Straik alive. He didn't know it yet, but his last hours were upon him.

Broderick would get the answers he sought from Duff's men, one way or another.

Alastair and James, a guard Broderick met when he first arrived at Straik, entered with another one of Duff's men and shoved him in the chair. The man sat straight as an arrow; his small eyes nervously darted between all three men.

"Yer name?" Broderick asked.

The man pursed his lips, not saying a word.

James approached him and kicked him in the chest with such force the man's arms windmilled as his chair fell backwards and crashed to the floor. Standing over him, James spat at the man.

"Laird MacLeod asked ye a question." James bent down and grasped his tunic. The man put his hands up in defense as he was hauled to his feet.

"Alright, alright! Dinna touch me." He scooted his arse across the floor until his back was against the wall.

Broderick folded his arms and waited. He couldn't possibly be folding this quickly.

"Seamus." He lowered his chin. "The name is Seamus."

"See. Was that so hard?" James stepped closer and Seamus shrank back, as if hoping the wall would open up and swallow him.

"Thank ye, James." Broderick dipped his head toward the other side of the room and the guard moved away from Seamus.

"Now that we've got that out of the way." Broderick looked down at him. "Where were ye before ye arrived at Straik?"

Seamus glared and mulled over what he was going to say. "'Twas east of here." He rubbed his chest where James's boot print could be seen on his tunic.

"Where?"

"I dinna ken exactly. Near Inverness."

The hairs on the back of Broderick's neck stood up. *Maggie.* She'd said her village was near Inverness. Hands fisted, he tamped down his anger, or he was going to beat this bastard to a bloody pulp before he got the information he needed.

"Did ye go into Inverness?" he asked.

"Nay." Seamus met Broderick's eyes and spit on the ground near him. "We raided a small village there. Yer father wanted to expand his lands. Thought the village would be easy picking. And, aye, 'twas verra much that." He sneered as he remembered the attack. "The lassies were ripe for the picking, if ye ken what I mean."

"Ye fecking bastard!" Before the bastard could blink, Broderick was on him, pounding his head into the ground.

Both James and Alastair pulled at his arms, trying to get him off Seamus, whose face was now a bloody mess.

"My laird. Cease!" Alastair commanded.

Broderick's anger overtook him and he only saw red. Breathing heavily, he pushed off the ground, and stormed to the other side of the room.

James lifted the unconscious Seamus by his armpits and dragged him from the room.

"Son," Alastair said quietly. "I ken yer ire, but ye need to control yourself. Ye're laird now, remember? That bastard deserved the beating, but ye canna lose yer temper. The clan had a laird like that in yer father and while he treated most of them kindly, he had his moments. Ye're bigger than that. Show yer men ye can lead without resorting to such actions."

"He just admitted to Maggie's attack, Alastair." Broderick nodded, licked his lips, and wiped the blood from his hands on his plaid. "That canna go unpunished."

"And it willna. But remember, Duff is who ye really want. He led the men there. Called out the orders."

"Aye," Broderick blew out a heavy breath.

Two more of Duff's men were brought in, but they remained silent. Broderick managed to contain his rage and sent them off to a cell unharmed.

The final man brought in was the shifty footed one he'd noticed earlier. He reeked of sweat and shuffled from one booted foot to another. The man spoke before Broderick asked him anything.

"Laird MacLeod." He turned. "Alastair."

"Donnie," Alastair acknowledged.

"Ye ken who he is?" Broderick looked to his mentor.

"Aye. Donnie used to work for yer father. He was supposed to be in the hunting party but disappeared a few days before Callum and Ewan were hunted down."

"Is that so?" Broderick's voice was laced with suspicion. "Where did ye go, Donnie?"

"My laird, I...uh...I," Donnie stuttered, unable to finish his sentence.

Broderick bent down until he was eye to eye with him, their faces just inches apart.

"Where in the hell did ye go?" His voice boomed with such force Donnie turned away.

"I, Duff, he..." His words came in torrent. "The plan was all his. I needed the coin and he paid weel. Weel enough for me to pay off my gaming debts."

"Ye betrayed my father and brother for some measly coin?" Broderick shoved him and he dropped onto the chair.

"They were going to hurt my family."

"So, instead ye hurt mine?" Broderick fumed.

"I didna ken he was going to kill them, my laird. I promise ye." Donnie dragged his forearm across his face to swipe away the beads of sweat. "He paid my debts in exchange for the hunting party's path."

"And then ye left Straik like a coward," Broderick scoffed.

"I needed to get away from my wife and daughters—to keep them from harm's way. I joined Duff's men. But, believe me, when I tell ye, I had no idea he was going to strike them down."

Broderick studied the quivering, sniveling man in front of him. He was sure Donnie spoke the truth. He didn't seem the type to think of anything so sinister himself.

"Ye will pay for yer betrayal," Broderick stated quietly.

"Aye." Donnie nodded and his head hung low.

"Alastair, put him with the rest of Duff's men. Ye and I have much to discuss."

The man was led out of the room and, assured he was alone, he slammed his fist into the table. "Hell!" he roared into the empty room.

He'd finally gotten the answers he'd sought, but he didn't feel any better than before.

Callum was a cruel bastard to Broderick and his mother, and Ewan had outgrown their childhood friendship and happily followed along in his father's footsteps. Even so, they didn't deserve an ending like that.

To be betrayed by one of the men ye had entrusted.

CHAPTER 17

"*My* lady," Una called from the other side of the door. "Laird MacLeod sent me up to stay with ye for the night."

Maggie unlatched the door and opened it just a crack, not letting her in.

"Una. There's nay need for that. I'm exhausted from the day's events and must confess that I will be retiring shortly. Ye dinna need to stay for that."

"But the laird..." she protested.

"I will deal with him in the morn'. Enjoy yer night. I will be fine."

Una looked unsure of herself, torn between Broderick's orders and Maggie's dismissal. After a few moments of Maggie not budging, she gave in, curtsied, and bid Maggie a good eve.

Maggie kept her ear to the door until the footsteps disappeared. She stripped off the nightdress and revealed the simple brown dress she wore underneath. She eyed the beautiful green cloak Broderick had given her, but it was too noticeable and would draw unwanted attention. Instead, she rummaged through the trunk at the end of her bed and pulled out a gray shawl with a hood. The drab garment would give her the anonymity she needed as she made her way through the halls and down to the dungeons.

Maggie pulled on her boots, grabbed her dagger off the table beside the bed, and slid it into her boot. After a last look around, she hurried to the door. It creaked as she swung it open and she froze, worried that everyone in the castle had heard. Breath held, she waited. When no one approached, she stuck her head out into the hall and looked both ways.

The flickering flames of the candles cast shadows along the walls and floor, making it look eerie, but the hall was clear.

Slipping out the door, she pulled it slowly shut and lifted the hood up to cover her hair and most of her face. Hopefully, no one would give her a second look and she could make it down to the dungeons without being stopped.

And pray tell, let her not run into Broderick, for surely, he would stop her.

Down the stairs she went with nary a second look. Passing the kitchens, she kept her head down, past the ale room and then down the narrow stone steps. They were damp and slick, so she placed a hand on the wall and tread carefully. Torches lit the way, and she heard voices as she neared the cells.

A guard stood at the end of the hall, watching the entrance to the cells.

What could she do? She needed him to go away. Another guard approached and she ducked into the shadows, her back flat against the cold stone.

Their deep voices rumbled off the stone walls, but she couldn't understand what they said. All she could make out were the words *ale* and *wench* before they clapped each other on the back and headed past her and up the stairs, mentioning the Great Hall as they passed.

She'd never been more thankful for darkness than she was when they walked by without discovering her there.

After she was sure they were gone and not coming back, she descended the stairs the rest of the way. In front of her, the dimly lit hall was lined by heavy doors on either side, each one equipped with a barred opening.

Slowly, she approached each door and dared a look inside. Nearing the end, she saw him—Duff—the beast who had forever changed her life.

Her heart quickened and she took a deep breath to calm herself, certain he would hear the beat of her heart as well as she heard it pounding in her ears. For a moment, she just stood there, staring at the bars, worried whether they would be strong enough to hold the monster within.

"Weel, weel, what have we got here?" Duff came closer and entwined his beefy fingers around the bars.

Though she knew he couldn't touch her, Maggie instinctively backed away. Trusting the bars would prevent him from reaching her.

But even in the dim light, she could see his evil sneer.

"'Twas ye earlier. I saw ye." He licked his lips. "And ye saw me. I could tell by the fear in yer eyes."

Even in the dim light, she could see his evil sneer and how much he was enjoying her discomfort.

Maggie lifted her chin. "Ye dinna frighten me." She was disappointed by the way her voice shook when she spoke.

"Ye survived the woods, I see." His leering eyes traveled over her body. "Impressive. I thought yer sorry body would have given up on ye, happy to be rid of ye."

His words were meant to hurt her. But he no longer had any power over her. Nay. She was now the one with all of the power.

"I've held onto this in the hopes 'twould help me learn ye identity." She reached into her pocket, pulled out the brooch, and held it up for him to see.

Duff reached out to snatch it from her hands, but the bars prevented him from doing so.

That solidified her courage.

"Ye canna hurt me anymore. I've waited all these weeks to learn yer name. Duff," she spat. "Ye've saved me the hassle of trekking the countryside hunting ye down."

"Ah, I see what is happening. Ye're in the laird's favor. I should have guessed ye couldna keep yer legs closed for long. Ye sure couldna when ye were with me."

"I did no such thing," she whispered.

"Dinna fool yerself, wench." His cruel laughter echoed off the stone walls. "Ye were begging me."

Against her better judgment she lashed out at him, clawing, scratching, anything to stop the vile words spewing from his mouth.

Duff's hand snaked through the bars to grip the back of her neck. With one strong yank, he knocked her head roughly against them.

Stunned, her ears ringing, she tried to back away, but his hand was tangled tightly in her hair. Blood ran from her nose and over her lip and she could taste the metallic tang in the back of her throat.

Not again.

This couldn't possibly be happening again. She twisted and tried to push against the bars, but his grip was too tight.

"I'm going to finish what I started." His meaty hands moved to her neck and he started to squeeze.

Dots appeared in her eyes as he tightened the pressure.

No!

He would not win. Not when he'd finally been caught.

She couldn't breathe, and she scratched at his hands trying to get him to loosen the pressure.

My dagger!

Her vision began to blur, she struggled to lift her leg as she reached down for her boot. She felt the soft hide rim. Almost there!

Duff cursed and spittle flew from his mouth as he crushed her throat.

Just. A. Wee. Bit. More.

Her fingertips brushed the hilt of the dagger. Just...a...bit...closer. She wrapped her hand around it and yanked it from her boot.

She raised her arm and blindly she swung with all her might in the direction of Duff's voice. Her grip strong, she closed her eyes, jammed the sharp steel into his flesh, and pulled it free.

"Ye fecking bitch!" he howled, and the pressure on her throat suddenly eased up as his hands fell away.

She dropped to the ground, throat sore, gasping for air. She scrambled away to the wall across from the cell, out of reach of the arm he'd stuck through the bars still grasping for her.

"Ye fecking whore. Where are ye?"

Her gaze flew to his face and she realized her dagger had struck him in the eye. His hand covered one side of his face and blood flowed between the fingers.

Maggie couldn't stop coughing and her breaths came quickly. So, this was how her life ended. At least she would die knowing she'd gotten Duff.

She desperately wanted Broderick, but could not catch her breath to call out for him.

The room began to spin and his face was the last thing she saw before everything went black.

BRODERICK KNOCKED on Maggie's door and waited. After he was done interrogating Duff's men, he'd gone to the kitchens and supped quickly before returning to her room. He was going to leave her alone for the night, until he'd seen Una walking the halls. He questioned her and learned Maggie had refused to let her accompany her for the night.

Nerves on edge, he'd raced up the steps and now he waited for Maggie to open the door. But there was no answer

"If ye dinna open the door, lass, I'm going to force it open." Thinking that would get her to let him in, he took a step back.

But the door didn't open.

Something was wrong. His heart in his throat, he lifted the handle and pushed the door open. The room was dark save for the fire that still held a low flame.

"Maggie?" he called out and entered the room. It was empty. "Where had she—bloody hell," he cursed as dawning washed over him.

He spun and ran out of the room and down the hall, taking the stairs two at a time."

"My laird," Alastair asked, concern darkening his features. "What has happened?"

"'Tis Maggie." Broderick called over his shoulder, not stopping to explain.

"Is she alright?"

"I dinna ken." He headed for the dungeons; Alastair following closely on his heels.

"Ye've taken my eye, ye bitch." Duff cursed as Broderick rounded the corner.

"No!" Broderick bellowed when he saw a form slumped

on the floor outside of Duff's cell. He rushed over to Maggie, he turned her onto her back, and bent to see if she breathed.

Relief flooded him as he felt her breath warm his skin.

Alastair knocked his sword against the bars to get Duff to back away.

"Maggie, lass, wake up, love." He held her face in his palms and noticed the trail of blood from her nose. Without letting Maggie go, he turned in Duff's direction.

"What did ye do?" he yelled. "What the hell did ye do to her?"

"I hope I finally killed the bitch." Blood covered Duff's face and hand.

It was as if all the air had been sucked out of the dungeons. Broderick's rage was too much to contain. His body shook with the need for vengeance. For Callum. For Ewan.

For Maggie.

He stood and unsheathed his sword. In one swift move he thrust it through the bars and felt it sink into the flesh of Duff's chest. Broderick withdrew it, opened his hand, and the sword clattered when it dropped to the ground.

Surprised at the sudden attack, Duff's good eye rounded as he clenched his chest before staggering back and collapsing in a heap.

Broderick hurried back to Maggie and lifted her to his chest.

She jerked awake, eyes panicked, she gasped and tried to suck in air. Her gaze softened when she saw Broderick, and she reached for him as she continued to cough.

"Shhh, lass, easy." He rocked her gently to calm her so she could get the air she desperately needed.

Broderick noticed the marks on her neck and cursed. Hugging her closely to him, he murmured soft words of reassurance until, finally, her coughing ceased.

He'd come too close to losing her.

"Duff…" No more than a whisper, the word hung in the air between them.

"Breathes no more."

Maggie smiled, winced, and lifted her hand to her nose. "My throat hurts." She rubbed at her neck. "But I'm so happy to see ye."

"I've ne'er been so scared in my life, lass. I couldna lose ye."

"And ye didna." She cradled her hand to his jaw then slid it to the back of his neck. She drew his head down to hers and pressed her lips to his. The pleasure of his lips against hers was such a wonderful contrast to the torment she'd suffered at Duff's hands.

She lowered her head and smiled. "We did it. He's dead."

"Aye. And most importantly, ye are no'."

"'Twas close, though." Swallowing, she scrunched her eyes.

"Ye're too strong for that." He skimmed her hair from her face. "I love ye, Maggie of unknown surname."

"Grant." She laughed, and Broderick had never heard anything so beautiful.

"Maggie Grant." He said, testing the name on his tongue. "Maggie Grant," he repeated. "I dinna want to be separated from ye e'er again. Marry me, lass?"

"Aye, my laird." Blessing him with a smile, she placed another kiss on his lips.

CHAPTER 18

*T*he days leading up to the wedding passed in a blur. The castle was abuzz with life and people were arriving from near and far to help Maggie and Broderick celebrate their union.

She never knew she could feel such joy. That just a glance from Broderick could have her insides melting. The relief that Duff was dead and could never harm her again, and that Broderick had avenged his father and brother's murder, had lifted an enormous weight from both of their shoulders.

They were suddenly free to enjoy life. To enjoy each other.

Maggie looked out over the crowd. There were so many names to remember. Broderick had a lot of friends. Each of them huge and looked just as strong as him. But they were kind and smiled broadly when they met her. Hopefully they wouldn't be offended if she happened to mix them up or call them by the wrong name. But she would do her best.

Tomorrow she would become Lady MacLeod. The thought of that happening was surreal. Maggie always believed she would marry one day, but it would be to one of the men in her village. Never, not even in her happiest times when her family was alive, did she ever have such a dream.

The fire blazed bright in the garden room, casting a warm shadow over the table Maggie was currently arranging. Due to the season, she didn't have any flowers available to dry, but she'd had fun drying leaves that she'd picked from the forest.

"My lady." Una peeked her head in the door. "We need to get ye ready for yer big day. A bath is being prepared for ye in yer chambers."

"Everyone is going through so much trouble." Maggie wasn't sure she'd ever get used to being fussed over.

"Laird MacLeod wants yer day to be special." Una moved to the fire and tamped it down, and the room was enveloped in darkness except for the single candle on the table.

"'Tis going to be special whether he makes such a fuss or no," Maggie insisted. "I tried talking him into a small quiet ceremony and he wasna having any of it."

"That sounds like Laird MacLeod." Una giggled. "I've heard he can be quite stubborn when he has his mind set to something."

Maggie nodded. "I agree with that." She clasped her hands together. "I canna believe I will be wed on the morrow."

With one last look at the garden room, Maggie followed Una out the door and up to her bedchamber. She eagerly awaited the spring when the gardens would begin to bud and come alive. She anticipated lots of time spent here in the future.

By the time dawn broke, Maggie was a bundle of nerves. She hadn't been able to sleep at all the night before. Worry that she would make a fool of herself in front of Broderick's friends and fellow clan members—soon to be her clan members as well.

She turned her head and gazed at the purple sky. It was going to be wonderful day. Snuggling into the throws, her eyes fell upon the gown hanging on her wardrobe. Someone had to have worked both day and night to complete it in time. Its intricate embroidery took a skilled hand. Thistles sewn in delicate stitches circled along the bottom border of the skirt, and a single fully bloomed thistle was centered in the bodice. The gown was one of the most beautiful things she'd ever seen.

"My lady?" A soft knock sounded, and Una's voice came through the door. "Are ye awake?"

"Aye," Maggie called, and the door swung open. Una entered followed by a handful of maids and finishing up the line was Orna.

The healer smiled widely as she came to sit on Maggie's bed. Reaching out her gnarled hand, she brushed her fingers through Maggie's hair.

"Ah, lass. 'Tis yer day and I couldna be happier for the two of ye. Found each other at exactly the right time, ye did. 'Twas fate." She patted Maggie's arm. "I ken ye were special, lass." Orna winked at her before pushing off the bed. "Ye'll make a lovely bride, Maggie."

"Thank ye for everything, Orna. If no' for yer care, I wouldna be here." Maggie took her hand and gave it a gentle squeeze. Without her healing skills and patience, Maggie would not find herself in this situation—getting ready to marry the man that showed her she was worth loving.

She couldn't wait to be married to Broderick and start their life together.

∾

AFTER WHAT SEEMED liked hours of primping, the time was here. Maggie placed her hand on her stomach to quell the fluttering happening inside her belly. On the other side of the large wooden door in front of her, was her husband to be, waiting for her to come through so they could state their vows and finalize their union.

"Ye look bonny, my lady," Una cooed. The maid had brushed her hair until it shone, and then continued to do so for a little longer before wrapping it around in a twist and fastening it with a hair pin that Broderick had sent to her chambers. The pin was made of bone and adorned with two red jewels. The piece had belonged to his mother. When he'd given it to Maggie, Broderick had said if Elspeth was alive today to see him wed, that she would want Maggie to have it.

It warmed her heart that he thought to give her something so special to him.

Maggie could hear the murmured conversations of those waiting inside the chapel. They'd all gathered to watch she and Broderick wed and the time had come. Trying not to think about how many people were inside, she took a deep, steadying breath, and walked through the door.

Immediately, Maggie's eyes locked with Broderick's and everything and everyone else fell away. Donning a plaid and linen shirt, his sword strapped at his side, he was the most handsome man she'd ever laid eyes on.

And he was hers.

His wide smile made her knees weak, and it was a struggle to take the final steps until he reached out his hand and drew her to his side.

"Ye are beautiful, lass," Broderick whispered in Maggie's ear when he bent to place a kiss on her cheek.

"Ye are quite dashing yourself, Laird MacLeod."

Maggie tried to concentrate on the words the priest spoke, but her focus was solely on Broderick.

"...according to God's holy ordinance; and thereunto I plight thee my troth." Broderick completed his vows, staring deeply into her eyes as he repeated after the priest.

With each word, he gave her hands a squeeze.

And then came Maggie's turn. "I, Maggie, take thee, Broderick, to be my wedded husband..." Somehow, she completed her vows, and the ceremony was over.

Broderick bent and captured her lips in a deep kiss that curled Maggie's toes and promised there was so much more to come for them. It was a good thing he had his strong arms wrapped around her, otherwise Maggie was sure she would have collapsed right there on the spot.

Cheers erupted and their guests congratulated them and clapped Broderick on the back as they passed. Maggie's face hurt from smiling so much at everyone as they made their way out of the chapel to the Great Hall. There, a grand feast had been laid out, along with dozens of pitchers of ale.

"'Tis so much," Maggie said in awe as she looked over dish after dish.

Broderick beamed. "Ye deserve naught less, Lady MacLeod." He raised his brows at the sound of her new name then captured her mouth in another kiss. "Let us eat. I canna promise ye I will want to stay long." He waggled his brows before stepping away to fill their trenchers with food.

The butterflies in her belly fluttered once more. She wasn't uneducated in what happened between a man and a woman, of course. And though she trusted Broderick completely, she was still nervous.

Carrying two overflowing trenchers of food, Broderick placed them on the table and took his seat beside Maggie at the dais.

"Are ye happy, lass?" He filled her chalice and then his and he drank deeply.

"I have ne'er been happier." She took a long swallow from her chalice.

The music started and cheers rose from the crowd. They sat side by side, watching their guests enjoy themselves as they danced and sang. Drank and ate.

Maggie could feel the heat emanating from Broderick's powerful body. He sat so close and yet, she wanted him to be closer. Every time he bent to whisper something in her ear, it sent shivers up and down her back. The flutters in her stomach had been replaced with wanting.

"I think we should retire to our bedchamber now," she said quietly.

Broderick's nostrils flared and his eyes darkened. "Ye dinna have to tell me twice, lass." He stood and held out his hand for her to accept.

She did and he pulled her to her feet. As they made their way through the Great Hall, they thanked those that traveled and bade them all a good eve.

Away from the festivities, the castle was quiet. Broderick stopped suddenly and pulled Maggie in for another breathtaking kiss. She wrapped her arms around his neck, and he pulled her even closer. After a few moments, he broke the kiss, both of them breathless in the best possible way.

"I have been waiting all day to do that." He winked and clasped her hand. "Come on, love. Our bedchamber awaits."

Biting her lip in anticipation, she let him lead her to his room.

BRODERICK'S CHAMBERS were exactly as Maggie imagined they would be. A huge, poster bed with an intricately carved trunk at the foot nearly took up one entire wall. A masculine wardrobe off to the side had the same intricate design as the trunk.

Ale had been brought up and he filled two cups and handed one to her, which she gladly accepted.

"Thank ye." She took a long sip, and pressed her lips together, suddenly feeling awkward and not knowing what to do with herself. Did she sit? Where? On the chair? The bed?

"Are ye nervous, lass?" Concern shadowed Broderick's handsome face.

"I would be lying if I said no," she answered truthfully.

"I will ne'er do anything to hurt ye, lass." He walked to the fireplace, leaned an arm on the mantle, and drank his ale.

She trusted he would do everything in his power to make sure of that. And she loved him for being so kind and considerate. Broderick would wait for as long as it was necessary, but she didn't want to live in fear.

This was her move to make.

Maggie placed her cup on the table and she wiped her palms on her skirts. She moved to the mantle, took Broderick's face in her hands, and pulled him down for a kiss. Tentatively, she skimmed her tongue along his lips. He relented on a sigh, and their tongues entwined.

Maggie's breath hitched and she had to remind herself to breathe, but the kiss left both of them gasping for air.

Broderick collapsed into the oversized chair in front of the fire, pulled her down, and settled her on his lap.

"Och, lass." He tucked a loose tendril of hair behind her ear, letting his fingers linger on her lobe. "What am I going to do with ye?

Electricity shot through her, and she shivered at the touch.

"I hope ye're going to love me."

He pulled the pin from the twist and watched as her hair tumbled down over her shoulders.

"Aye. I already do." He picked up a strand of her hair, bought it to his nose and inhaled. "Lavender. The scent suits ye well, lass."

"I ken ye love me." She turned in his lap. "I meant ye will love me. Er…" Bother, she was making a mess of this. How could she be so forward and so meek at the same time?

Broderick raised a brow at her, amusement brightening his eyes.

"Are ye going to make me say it?" she asked.

"I've no idea what ye are referring to, lass." One corner of his mouth twitched.

She playfully slapped at his chest, but he caught her hand and kissed each fingertip.

Maggie watched, as he moved from one finger to the next, before placing his lips on her palm.

Oh, but the room was getting hot.

"I like that," she whispered, tracking his movements.

"Do ye?"

She nodded.

He gave her hand a tug, and she collapsed against his chest, their faces inches apart.

"What do ye want, lass?" Broderick asked quietly, his eyes never leaving hers, as his hands stroked circles across her back.

"Ye. I want ye, Broderick MacLeod."

He captured her mouth with his, crushing his lips against hers in the most pleasant way and when he broke the kiss, she was left gasping for air.

Shifting her around, he tucked his one arm beneath her legs, the other behind her back, and stood.

She squealed and held tightly to his shoulders.

He stopped beside the bed and set her down. "Are ye sure, lass? Ye can tell me no at any point."

"I am sure. I've been ready for this since yer first gentle kiss because I knew in that moment ye would never hurt me." She turned so her back was to him. "I need help with the ties of my gown."

She sucked in a breath at the feel of his fingertips brushing her skin as he carefully tugged and loosened the ties one by one. He seemed to be moving excruciatingly slow and she bit her tongue to keep from ordering him to hurry up.

He kissed the side of her neck, causing goosebumps to skitter across her body. Then he slipped the gown off her shoulders, down her arms, and let the material fall and pool at her feet.

Maggie stood there, wearing only her shift and her stockings, and worried about what happened next. Would she be frightened? She mustered her courage, turned in Broderick's arms and lifted her chin to see his face.

His gaze traveled over her and she saw nothing but love in his eyes. She'd been worried unnecessarily.

Reaching up, she untied the laces at his neck. She grabbed the hem, and he leaned forward she so could pull it over his head. Her eyes widened at the sight of his massive chest and the array of scars marring his flesh in various places.

"Are all of these from battle?" She lightly traced the patterns of the warm, raised skin.

"Aye." He captured her hand in his. "If ye keep touching me, lass, I willna make it long." He gently pushed her onto the bed, and she sank into the throws.

Broderick drew down her stockings one leg at a time and tossed them onto the pile of her gown. Gently, he placed his lips on her ankle and continued to drag kisses up the inside of her leg, until he neared the apex of her thighs.

She'd never felt such a sensation and sucked in her breath.

"Breathe, lass." He smiled devilishly as he looked up at her from that spot, his face so close to her core.

Maggie exhaled the breath she hadn't realized she'd been holding and when she did, he darted his tongue out and licked her most sensitive flesh.

"Oh!" Her back arched of its own accord.

Broderick chuckled against her, vibrating through her core. He nipped at her flesh and then licked the spot again. As he continued his slow torture, pressure unlike anything she'd ever experienced built in Maggie's belly. Tightening. Coiling.

Broderick dipped a finger between her folds, and Maggie moaned at the sensation. He added another and slowly worked them in and out as he continued to lave at her apex.

Reaching down, she fisted her hands in his hair, afraid she would spin off the earth if she let go.

He moved his fingers faster, quickening the pace of his tongue and the pressure was too much for Maggie to take. Her hips lifted off the bed and she couldn't stop the whimpers that escaped her mouth in an unending stream. Her body was surely going to burst into oblivion.

"Let it go, lass," Broderick murmured against her.

She gave in to her body's urges and let go, releasing an explosion of epic proportions. Wave after wave, she basked in the pleasure that flowed through her.

Broderick joined her on the bed and wrapped her in his arms.

"I've ne'er…" Maggie snuggled atop his chest as she tried to come back down to earth.

He stroked her hair and placed a kiss on her forehead. "I love ye, lass." He captured her mouth in another soul-crushing kiss and she could taste herself on his lips.

They slowly ended the kiss and she ran her hands over his chest, his arms, and pulled him closer. "I love ye, too."

"There's more where that came from." He grasped handfuls of her shift from where he'd pushed it up around her waist, lifted it over her head, and tossed it across the room.

Broderick rolled so she was beneath him and he stared at her breasts. His nostrils flared as he bent and sucked a nipple into his mouth. Then moved to her other breast and did the same.

"I want to see ye." She reached out and tugged on his plaid. It only seemed fitting that if she were to be naked, he should be as well.

"I thought ye would ne'er ask." He climbed from the bed and instantly her skin pimpled at the coolness of his absence.

Maggie couldn't take her eyes from Broderick as he unwrapped the plaid and bared his body to her. Her eyes widened at the sight. His muscles rippled and contracted, and his manhood stood erect, garnering her full attention. He looked hard as iron.

Joining her on the bed once again, he lay on his side and tucked her into him. His fingers lazily trailing over her arms, down her side, around her breast. His slow, gentle movements had her insides warring. She wanted more. She wanted him to touch her in her most intimate places as he'd done before.

She pulled him towards her, placed her lips on his chest, and smiled against his warm skin.

"Are ye ready, lass?" Concern laced his voice.

"Aye, my husband. I'm no' scared."

Broderick rolled until he was settled between her thighs. Maggie could feel his length pressing at her opening, and still he held back.

"Make me yers, Broderick MacLeod." She smiled and framed his face with her hands.

"As ye wish, Lady MacLeod." Slipping his hand between them, he guided himself to her entrance and slowly pushed himself into her.

Maggie gasped, surprised by the fullness of his length. He hinged back and pushed forward again, going deeper this time. He repeated that movement until he filled her completely and their bodies melded into one.

A perfect fit.

"Och, lass. Ye feel like heaven."

She answered with a moan, because she couldn't get herself to form words. She was in a state of bliss she'd never known was possible.

As he began pumping his hips, her belly tightened again. And when he reached his hand between them and placed pressure on her little nub of pleasure, she lost complete control of her body.

Broderick pumped faster as he whispered her name across her ear. Her body coiled, tighter, tighter, tighter until it blew apart into a thousand tiny shards.

He stiffened and ground out her name before collapsing beside her. Not wanting to separate them he took her with him.

It took some time for her breath to calm and return to normal. When her eyes met Broderick's, they were crinkled into a smile.

"I liked that verra much."

"I did, too." He returned her smile and rubbed his hands along her back. "Here, get under the throws so ye dinna catch a chill." He maneuvered them so they could crawl under the covers, and she once again snuggled into his strong arms.

"I dinna e'er want to leave ye and this room." She looked up at him. "Can we stay here for eternity?"

"If that is what ye want." Broderick laughed.

Maggie sighed, knowing it wasn't possible, but wishing it all the same.

"I love ye, husband." She pushed up on her elbows and met his eyes. "I've ne'er been happier."

"Maggie, love. I knew the moment I found ye in the woods that ye were a warrior. Strong and fierce. I love ye with all my heart, wife." He kissed her forehead. "Now, get some rest, so we can do that all o'er again."

Maggie giggled, the excitement of the day and bliss she'd just experienced was catching up to her, making her eyes heavy. She could now sleep easy, and when she woke up, her husband would make her see stars again.

And she couldn't wait.

EPILOGUE

*T*hree weeks later

Maggie stirred in Broderick's arms. Dawn was breaking and he had a busy day ahead of him, but he didn't want to leave the warmth of their bed. If he had his way, he'd spend the rest of his days in this very position, loving on his wife, and basking in her essence.

"Good morn," Maggie whispered and placed a soft kiss on his chest.

His body reacted immediately. Growling, he flipped Maggie onto her back in one swift move and brought his lips down to hers. He took his time savoring her mouth as he settled himself between her legs.

"I want to wake up like this every morn," he mumbled against her lips.

Sighing, she wrapped her legs around his waist, and taking her cue, he entered her in one thrust. Her breath caught and he smiled. He'd never tire of the look on her face whenever he was inside her. The way she completely lost herself in the throes of their ecstasy.

He moved his hips slowly, taking his time, but Maggie wanted none of it.

She skimmed her fingers down his sides and down to his arse. She pulled him down to her, urging him to move faster.

"Och, lass, ye'll be the death of me." *What a death that would be.*

"And ye'll be the death of me, if ye dinna quicken yer pace." She bit at his neck, then licked the spot.

His couldn't deny his wee wife of her wishes and did as she asked. Pumping his hips faster, he reveled in her softness.

Her hands on his shoulders now that she got what she wanted, she curled her nails into his skin—a bite of pain with the pleasure—and he loved it.

Grinding his hips into her, he felt her tightening around him, and he slipped his hand between them, and stroked her pleasure nub, sending her over the edge. Her body clamped down on his cock and with a final thrust, he found his release, and they rode the wave together.

Their bodies spent, gasping for breath, Broderick rolled to the side, and trailed his fingers along Maggie's belly. She shivered and blessed him with a smile.

"Stay?" she asked, biting her lip.

"I wish I could, lass." He nuzzled her neck. "There's naught more that I want to do, but Alastair and I have something to do we canna delay any longer." Throwing off the covers, he stood and quickly dressed. "Dinna fash, love," he bent over and kissed her one last time before leaving to meet his mentor. "We will finish this later." Patting her bottom through the throws, he gave her a devilish grin. Promises of pleasures to come.

Closing the door behind him, he took a deep breath. Leaving Maggie in their bed was one of the hardest things he had to do. These past weeks, he'd severely neglected his Amadán duties.

He descended the stairs and walked toward the Great Hall. Una passed him in the hall and gave him a quick curtsy.

"Is Lady MacLeod awake?" Una asked.

"Aye, she should break her fast." He adjusted his tunic.

Una nodded. "I shall bring her some food immediately, my laird."

"Thank ye, Una."

She hurried towards the kitchens and Broderick knew she would see to Maggie's needs while he was gone.

"Ye're looking like ye've had a satisfying morn," Alastair quipped, appearing out of nowhere.

"I'm a verra happy man," he chuckled.

Alastair had wanted to see he and Maggie unite from the moment Broderick had found her that night in the woods that cold, dark night.

"I've no doubt." His mentor lowered his voice. "Ye ready to do this?"

"Aye, 'tis past time I take care of the things I've been putting off."

In the stables, Broderick and Alastair saddled their horses.

"Goliath, ye big beastie." Broderick ran his hand down his horse's black mane. "Ye ready for a ride?" Goliath huffed and stomped his hoof.

The men mounted, made their way out of the stables and headed in the direction of the woods. There were no crofts in this direction and after some time, Alastair halted his horse. Broderick pulled on Goliath's reins, bringing him to a stop as well.

Studying the woods, Broderick saw naught but trees. No paths. Nothing to give any hint that there was anything but forest here.

"We're almost there," Alastair said.

"Ye canna tell me where we are going?" Broderick raised a questioning brow.

"'Tis best to show ye." A huge grin broke out on Alastair's face, giving him the appearance of a much younger man.

The two of them had attended many secret meetings with other members of the Amadán, but never on MacLeod lands. Broderick had refused to step foot on them.

A whoop sounded from behind a copse of trees and Alastair kicked his horse into a trot, following the sound.

Broderick did the same and continued on until they came upon Doughall Munro, standing tall in a clearing in the woods. His long black hair was tied at the nape, and he was wearing the red and green colors of his clan.

"Lewis." He dipped his head in greeting before turning to Broderick. "Laird MacLeod," he said, holding back his laughter.

"Aye, aye," Broderick said as he dismounted his horse, and the two men shook hands. "Laugh all ye want."

"I'm no' laughing." The man couldn't keep a straight face to save his life. "Ye must admit 'tis funny finding yerself laird after all the years ye've spent stating ye never wanted to be one. I've only heard good things in my travels, so it seems ye've taken to the role just fine. And your Maggie is lovely." His tone became more serious. "I'm glad ye've found the happiness ye sought for so long, Broderick."

"Thank ye." He surveyed the area, deep in MacLeod lands.

The clearing was surrounded by dense woods and well hidden. Not one people would just stumble upon. Large, flat stones had been arranged in a circle and each of the men sat on one.

Doughall pulled a skin of ale from a sack, and after popping off the top and taking a sip, he passed it to Broderick.

The ale tasted faintly of heather but was pleasant enough.

He offered the skin to Alastair and watch as he took a sip and handed it back to Doughall.

"Is this where ye meet when ye call the Amadán to Straik?" Broderick asked.

"Aye, ye refused to come home so other arrangements were made for our meetings with ye."

There was no heat or accusation in Alastair's words, yet Broderick still felt a spear of guilt.

"I see the fault in my stubbornness." He sighed. "I shouldna have been so thick-headed. I apologize."

He had been selfish all these years to expect Alastair and his warrior brothers make special accommodations merely to placate his issues with the past. It wasn't right and he should have thought of that earlier. Of course, if he refused to go home where Alastair lived, they would have to set different meeting places.

"We all have our demons, Broderick." Alastair stated solemnly speaking from personal experience. "Sometimes, it takes us a long time to lay them to rest. What's done is done and we canna change the past. We can only move forward."

"Ye're right." Broderick nodded. "Let us discuss the mission."

"Doughall, as ye're aware, Broderick was on his way to Inverness when he was called back to deal with the matters here at Straik. Ye've just finished another successful mission, and since our other brothers are tied up with their own missions at the moment, I'm assigning it to ye."

Doughall rubbed the stubble on his chin, before nodding in acceptance. "Tell me what I need to know and consider it done."

An hour later, Doughall had all the details to carry out his next mission and the men said their goodbyes.

"Give yer bonny wife my well wishes. Until we meet

again." Doughall brought his fist to his chest and mounted his horse.

"Watch yer back, brother." Broderick warned.

"Always. Now return to yer wife. Ye've just married and should be in her arms right now."

"Och, aye. 'Tis where I'm headed next." And he meant it.

As much as he loved being an Amadán warrior, he couldn't imagine leaving Maggie for weeks, even months at a time while he completed missions for Alastair. Nay, as agreed upon, he would help Alastair lead the band of warriors from Straik, while hopefully, if it was meant to be, raising his family.

"If ye'll excuse me, since we are done here, I've a wife that is anxiously awaiting my return." He settled himself on Goliath's back and dug his heel into his ribs.

Doughall and Alastair's whoops and hollers echoed in Broderick's ears as he navigated his way back out onto the path that would lead him back to Straik castle and into Maggie's arms. A place he never wanted to leave.

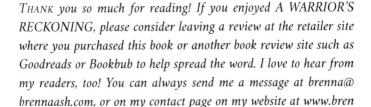

THANK you so much for reading! If you enjoyed A WARRIOR'S RECKONING, please consider leaving a review at the retailer site where you purchased this book or another book review site such as Goodreads or Bookbub to help spread the word. I love to hear from my readers, too! You can always send me a message at brenna@ brennaash.com, or on my contact page on my website at www.bren naash.com.

ALSO BY BRENNA ASH

Historical Romance

SCOTTISH ROGUES OF THE HIGH SEAS Series

A PIRATE'S TREASURE
A PIRATE'S WRATH

Paranormal Romance

DARK MOOR GUARDIANS Series
A KISS OF STONE

Contemporary Romance

PEBBLE HARBOR Series
SECOND CHANCES

ABOUT THE AUTHOR

Brenna Ash is addicted to coffee and chocolate. When she's not writing, she can be found either poolside reading a book, or in front of the TV, binge-watching her favorite shows, *Outlander, Bridgerton,* and all things true crime. She lives in Florida with her husband and a very, very spoiled cat named Lilly. She loves to interact with her readers on social media. Please feel free to follow her at the following platforms:

www.facebook.com/BrennaAshAuthor
www.twitter.com/brenna_ash
www.pinterest.com/ash0182
www.instagram.com/BrennaAshAuthor

To stay up to date on all things Brenna Ash, including book news, release dates and contest info, please sign-up for her newsletter on her website.

www.BrennaAsh.com

Printed in Great Britain
by Amazon

19502185R00133